The Governess Teaches A Duke

WAYWARD DUKE ALLIANCE

STEFFY SMITH

Steffy Smith Books

First published in Australia in October 2025 by Steffy Smith

Text copyright © Steffy Smith, 2025

Edited by Juicy Details Romance Editing, 2025

Cover Art by Mandy Koehler Designs

ISBN (Print) 978-1-7637632-2-7

ISBN (E-book) 978-1-7637632-0-3

 Formatted with Vellum

Can you share with me what you find so amusing?"

"Your disdain for Mr Whiskers! What prejudice do you hold against cats?"

"Their attitudes. They lack obedience and humility, and the way they make eye contact, with such impertinence. It raises my ire."

"Yes, cats are full of unapologetic confidence—which is personally what I adore! Though I now understand why you react in such a way to Mr Whiskers. You are unyielding when it comes to your views, your needs, and your wants, and luckily for you, you can be."

Maribel lowered her head to daintily sniff the steamed mackerel emitting the scent of fennel and mint and smiled.

"This smells divine."

"You are right, Maribel. I am unyielding. My wants, my needs. And what I need and want right now —is you."

Prologue

London, 1815

"Your Grace, I have news. News that will bring you joy, and news, Your Grace, that will bring sorrow, for which I am most sorry."

Thomas Denby, the Duke of Avondale, already knew what news the doctor brought. He had heard the cries of his staff. The hushed but distressed whispering of the doctor and his butler. And most distinctly, the wails of a newborn child. His child.

"In a single moment, I have gained a child and lost a wife. Is this the news you speak of?" Thomas's voice was hollow, and he barely recognised it. Only wed a year and so soon with child, the time had passed quickly, and he had been happy. Content. Blessed. To wed and produce an heir was one's duty, and his sweet bride Anne had been raised to be a duchess. Her own father was a duke. Now he was widowed and solely responsible for this new life.

"I am so very sorry, Your Grace. My heart weeps in sorrow."

"Thank you, Doctor. Is the child a boy or girl?"

"A girl, Your Grace. A healthy and beautiful baby girl."

He heard the slight tremor in the doctor's voice, and he could not blame the man. It would be hypocrisy to do so, as when he had heard the word girl—to his shame—he had been disappointed. Wallowing in the selfish moment a little longer, he closed his eyes and breathed deeply, trying to rationalise his thoughts. A girl meant he would need to remarry, to try to produce a male heir. The next Duke of Avondale.

Slowly, Thomas opened his eyes and saw the doctor still standing there, watching him solemnly. Thomas gave him a curt nod of dismissal. There was no will in him to extend any polite courtesy. Walking over to the table, he poured himself a claret, swallowing the bitter liquid in one motion.

"Your Grace?" He turned to see his butler, Mr Jones, in the door.

"What is it?" he asked through gritted teeth.

"The babe has settled, if you would like to meet her?" he heard the hopeful plea, and instead of feeling shamed by his coldness, it emboldened him.

"No. Please inform the rest of the staff that I wish to be alone until I advise otherwise."

He heard Mr Jones walk away and picked up the bottle of claret to pour himself a second drink, but before he could do so, a raging fire erupted inside him, and he threw the bottle at the wall with a roar of anger. The shattering glass echoed through the haze of his fury. Or was it grief? All he knew was that, in a single moment, he had been given one life and had had another taken away. And now he alone was responsible for this new life. His daughter. What did he know about raising a daughter?

Chapter One

nglish Countryside, 1822

Miss Maribel Lewisham slammed shut the heavy book she had been reading from. The resounding smack echoed throughout the room, and the two boys in front of her fell silent. Her younger brothers stopped pushing each other and looked up at her.

"We are sorry, Mari." It was bad enough to have one set of those sweet brown eyes turned up at her in an apology, but both was too much, and she shook her hand fondly at the incorrigible pair. Being the sister of five brothers, she had seen this look many a time. The twins, Frederick and Richard, were bundles of energy but their terrible attention span only helped her work on the patience she would need as a governess. As she had with their brothers, who were now of age to be working men themselves. John was now a clergyman, Matthew was studying to be a solicitor, and Liam had joined the church.

"I will accept your apology if one of you can recount what I was just talking about."

Looking to each other, they whispered for a moment before responding.

"You were reading a story about the Greeks battling," offered Richard.

"Close—"she withheld an eyeroll"—but not quite. I was reading you a piece of Roman history, from their greatest statesman, Cicero, and his time in exile."

"If you start again, we promise to listen this time, Mari," Frederick assured her with his sweet smile.

"Very well. Sit down, and I will begin."

Opening the book, she flicked through to find the page she had been on.

"Mari, a letter has come for you."

This announcement from her mother made her forget her own decorum, and she dropped the book to the floor with a thud as she squealed in delight.

"I am coming, Mother. Please let it be an offer of employment!"

Running to find her mother, she almost collided with the poor woman when she entered the kitchen.

"Slow down, Mari, where are your manners?" Mrs Lewisham scolded.

Snatching up the letter, she saw that the heavy wax seal was rich and imprinted with a lion crest. She ripped the parchment open and then quickly closed it in excitement.

"It is from the duke!"

Maribel had applied to a governess role for the Duke of Avondale's daughter and had been eagerly awaiting a response. Pausing for a moment, she tried to calm herself, her good sense reminding her it may not be the answer she wanted. Taking a deep breath, she opened the letter and read the contents.

Miss Maribel Lewisham,
The Duke of Avondale, Thomas Denby,
seeks your employment in the position of

governess to his daughter. Please come prepared, including any belongings you need, as if a suitable fit, you will be required to start immediately…

An interview? With a duke? She had assumed a steward or the butler would be conducting the interview. The duke himself? And to move in straight away!

"Mari, what is it?" her mother asked anxiously, knowing how much this news would mean to her.

'The Duke of Avondale wants to interview me. He, himself. A duke!"

"Freddy, our Mari is going to meet a duke," Richard stated in awe.

"This is wonderful news, Maribel! Wipe the concern from your face. You are educated and well-mannered. And he may be a duke, but title aside, he is just a human. Like you. Like us."

Maribel nodded her head slowly. Her mother spoke true, of course.

But it did not make her any less nervous. She was aware of the Duke of Avondale for reasons aside from his need of a governess. The women of the ton found him a most desirable marriage partner, and season after season, he had not taken a bride, despite being widowed for the last eight years. She had heard he was charming and attractive but also cold and rigid. That was the natural state of a duke though, was it not? Maribel hugged her mother and brothers, telling them she needed to go prepare, but really, she wanted a moment alone. As eager as she was for this opportunity, the reality of leaving her family was starting to dawn on her. Throwing herself on her bed, she looked up at the wooden ceiling and tried to calm her racing thoughts.

One at a time, she told herself, always frustrated when she could not catch a single thought. Instead, when her emotions heightened, they flurried around her mind like a blizzard. Shaking her head with such vigour that her bonnet flew off, she took the opportunity to knead her scalp, massaging away some of the tension.

She heard a self-important meow and looked to the door as Mr Whiskers strolled in, meeting his haughty expression.

"Mr Whiskers, I shall take you with me."

The black feline, short-haired and sleek, had been her closest confidante for six years. She had found the kitten asleep in the barn atop a bale of hay. When she had gently nudged him, one eye had opened and he had released a menacing meow. They had been inseparable ever since.

"Enough with the dillydallying! It is time to prepare."

Mr Whiskers was well-accustomed to her change in moods and paid no mind as she went from procrastinating to pacing and gathering her wits. The moment she had been waiting for had arrived.

Chapter Two

The Duke of Avondale, Thomas Denby, was not a man known for his patience. Nor was he reasonable. And he simply did not care. In the years since he had been widowed, he had made his peace with the reality of raising his daughter alone. But by raise, he really meant oversee. She was a girl after all. And he loved the sweet child, impish as she was, always wreaking havoc throughout his halls. All he sought was a governess with a spine of steel, who would not faint at the sight of a worm on her pillow or cry tears of frustration at dealing with a stubborn child. Each previous governess—there had been four now—had been interviewed by his steward. This time, Thomas would be doing the interview himself to ascertain the mettle of the woman and not waste his time. He pictured a bland woman, having assumed she would be plain, otherwise why be a governess. Even a middle-class maiden of beauty could marry into a comfortable life. Instead of being in London, he was waiting for this gentlewoman. If she met his requirements, he could continue his social life in London soon enough.

Thomas sat at his desk, tapping the heavy wood with

impatience. He had said noon, and according to the pocket watch that lay open before him, it was almost that time. It was not a positive sign that she lacked the good sense to arrive early instead of right on time. Scowling, he stood and paced the length of the room. How very impertinent she must be!

A few moments later, there was a rap on the door. "Enter."

He did not turn immediately, wanting to calm his frustration.

"Your Grace, I have Miss Maribel Lewisham here to be interviewed for the position of governess."

"Thank you, that will be all."

Footsteps left the room, and the door shut.

Then, in the silence of the room, a throat cleared.

Thomas knew it was rude that he still had his back to the woman, nor had he greeted her properly, but to clear her throat? Impertinence!

Turning around with his glare firmly in place, he faced her. His frustration was quickly replaced by surprise, and his brows lifted at the attractive girl that stood before him. He was equally dumbfounded by her disapproving look.

"Your Grace, as announced, I am Miss Maribel Lewisham and here for the role of governess. Shall we sit?"

Before he could respond, she walked towards the desk, her short legs taking long, confident strides against the floor. Thomas shook his head in disbelief.

Who did this chit think she was, addressing him so cooly and with such evident disapproval?

He stomped towards the desk, sat in the chair opposite her, and glowered. The impertinent woman did not even blink. Her warm chestnut eyes held his gaze.

"How old are you?"

"I am twenty years."

"What experience do you have? If any."

"I have no experience working for an employer, however I have played governess to my younger brothers, as well as to three elder, which I assure you only strengthened my resolve."

"Where did you learn and study?"

"I spent time in Bath with Miss Francine Porter, an esteemed governess who provides training, and I also received a fairly advanced education as a child."

"What can you teach?"

"I can teach fluent French, reading and writing skills, simple arithmetic, many historical topics, and for the young lady, needlepoint, water painting, and all social expectations."

"Do you have any other skills? Musical perhaps?

His daughter had gone through many a piano teacher, and he was determined to see her master at least one instrument.

"I do not possess any natural talent, but I can teach the pianoforte."

Her tone was polite but the answers were direct, firm. It was as if she was a teacher and he was a student in this exchange. The only thing keeping him from reprimanding her for her lack of civil address was his recognition of her comportment. Perhaps she would be able to handle his daughter after all.

"If I may, Your Grace, can I have some details about your daughter. What is her name and age?"

Her tone implied she found it improper that he had not yet provided this information. That same air he had been momentarily impressed with now induced annoyance.

"My daughter's name is Clara. She is seven. Is there anything else you need to know, Miss Lewisham?"

The slight pink tinge that touched her cheeks gratified him. Finally, a sliver of a reaction. Looking her over, he spied what appeared to be luscious curves under her muted clothing.

"Do you have any other questions?"

"Am I permitted to bring my cat?"

His jaw dropped. *She wants to bring a cat?* He could not stand felines. They had a smug, entitled air about them. His mother had owned one, and he had hated the damn species ever since. "You may not."

He had not meant to sound so cold and stiff, noting her lips had pressed into a thin line at his response.

"As you wish, Your Grace."

Refraining from clearing his throat to relieve the awkward silence, he stood.

"Consider yourself employed, Miss Lewisham. Someone will attend to you shortly."

Striding out of the room, he again had to stop himself, this time from looking back. He could feel her sharp gaze boring into him as he closed the door behind him. She had provoked something in him—a heady mix of excitement and frustration—and it suddenly dawned on him that perhaps hiring a governess who stirred his loins was not a wise decision.

Chapter Three

The door had closed gently, but it had left a cacophony ringing through her head as she stared at the spot where he had exited. Duke or not, Thomas Denby was an extremely rude man. His handsomeness was no consolation for his poor manners. The streaks of grey in his dark hair only made him more attractive, she begrudgingly admitted to herself. And Maribel could plainly see that this man had never heard the words *no* or *be nice* in his life. His glower was indeed quite haughty, but she had received far worse from Mr Whiskers. And thinking of her precious boy, she could not help but feel crushed at the thought of being parted from him. How could she possibly explain? He was far more intelligent than any other of his species and would surely see returning home as a betrayal. This opportunity to work for a duke, no matter how disagreeable, was too good to pass up. She would have to accept it.

Recalling the size of the country estate, it dawned on her that Mr Whiskers could stay and would just need to be kept out of sight. Surely both of these too high in the instep males would not cross paths. Mr Whiskers would not care for the duke's arrogance either. Impatiently, she rose and shook out her arms as she turned her gaze to the room. The furnishings were rich–newer Hepplewhites blended in with antique pieces she imagined had been in his family for decades, if not longer. The Aubusson carpet underneath her feet was soft and comforting as she slowly stepped around the study. She had always had an eye for furnishings, having paid keen attention in her training about working for the aristocracy. A childhood friend was now a maid for an earl and had detailed the house and where its contents had been made, and Maribel had revelled in the knowledge of it all.

As she continued her examination, it began to dawn on her that, while everything was rich, it was uninviting. The room was cold and austere, all shades of brown and white without any colour. The portraits on the wall depicted unsmiling people, and despite it being common practice, she could tell these people would have rarely smiled. The duke clearly came from a long line of stern ancestry—people of wealth and privilege who demanded respect and obedience. Her mind stuck on obedience as she trailed her fingers over a canonical metal ornament and silently seethed. The way he had spoken to her had indeed been master like. As if she were an obedient dog.

How dicked in the nob do I sound at this moment? I have secured a role as a governess for a Duke where our class divide is immeasurable, and I have taken insult at this very fact. I am the hired help. This is how I will be spoken to, how I will be treated. If he asks me to hop on one foot, I shall say yes. If he turns his back on me while I am mid-sentence, I will merely close my mouth.

Maribel was too practical to dwell on this further and instead embraced her earlier impish impulse.

I will not send Mr Whiskers away! I will keep him here and out of sight, and if his grace comes across him, he will have to pass as any stray! Surely there is many a stray cat on the grounds.

Feeling more in control, she turned back to her seat when a tap on the door made her turn. The butler opened the door and said he would show her to her rooms where her belongings would be waiting. Here was another person in this home who it seemed had not learned to smile, as his face was a stern duplicate of his employer's. Maribel had known she would miss her family for many reasons, but one she had not counted on was so simple.

Smiles.

Chapter Four

Thomas stood in the parlour staring out the window as his staff brought in Miss Lewisham's belongings. Three travel trunks, which surprised him. Why did she have so many things? He saw something black dart into the bushes. A vole? They weren't black though. Thomas reflected on their encounter and the feeling it had left him with. Eager, was that the right emotion? He was feeling eager for her to settle so he could leave. He would allow a few days to ensure Clara was not proving too much for her. But something niggled in the back of his mind, taunting him that he was eager to see more of the impertinent Miss Lewisham. He was still in disbelief at her forthrightness—she clearly was not accustomed to dealing with anyone of rank. And she needed to learn her place as his employee.

This side of her would prove beneficial in dealing with Clara, for she would not tremble at the idea of being firm. Something his wayward daughter surely needed. Miss Lewisham held strong promise in that regard, even if it meant she would try his own patience from time to time. Asking if she could bring a pet? As if she was coming to stay at a menagerie. *Country girls*, he thought, shaking his head. A type of woman he was not accustomed to dealing with. Well-bred ladies of high social standing and high-class courtesans of exquisite skill. These were the kind of women he was familiar with. Opposite sides of the social ladder, but they had one thing in common. Obedience. Knowing when to speak and when not to. His departed wife, brief as their marriage had been, had been skilled in that art. He knew many ladies of the ton who did not share those values, and while he found the stories of his fellow peers humorous, he was glad to not have to deal with these dramas.

His close peer, the Earl of Brookfield, kept him apprised of the on-dit. Fingering the signet ring on his left hand, a symbol of their unspoken alliance, he wondered what he had missed so far in London, where the season was underway. He knew he had missed the opening opera and Almack's. In comparison to the thrill Miss Lewisham's arrival had given him, the season now paled. While he was in London, she would be here, with her big brown eyes and soft curves, attempting to chasten his insolent child. Never before had he had an impulse to observe the day-to-day activities of a governess and his daughter. Realising he had the next few days to quell his curiosity, he was glad.

"Bronson, send Clara here to me. And some refreshments —something sweet to temper the news of a new governess."

His footman hurried off to provide instruction to the housekeeper, and Thomas stretched his neck, enjoying the slight crack of tension released. Dealing with his daughter required additional patience he never gave anyone else.

Clara, my sweet child, come sit here," he said, patting the seat next to him. The fair-haired angelic-looking girl sat down with a beaming smile.

"Father! I was wondering when I would see you today."

A maid came in with a tray of sugar plums and a glass of milk, and Clara's blue eyes widened with joy at the sweet treats placed before her.

Not minding her manners, as usual, she snatched one of the plums and plopped it into her mouth. Withholding a sigh, he turned to her with his full attention.

"I employed a new governess today—her name is Miss Lewisham. I think you will like her. She is different from the others. Younger in age and perhaps more interesting to take your lessons with."

Clara's face immediately soured. Her arms were now crossed, and her lips pouted as she gave him a petulant stare.

"Father, I do not need a governess. Why must I have one when I do not need a mother?"

Thomas held back a sigh. This was the same question she asked each time a new governess was appointed. Clara had no qualms about him not remarrying—if anything, he imagined she would take it quite poorly. But the clever child had now drawn this conclusion, and the matter was settled in her mind.

"Clara, we have discussed this many, many times. A governess is not a mother, you are correct. And even if your mother was here with us, you would still need a governess. You must be educated, your talents honed, and your manners polished. One day I will present you at court. One day you will have crowds of men clamouring for your hand in marriage. And all the lessons you learn now will prepare you."

"Marriage! I am never getting married father. You are not married, so why do I have to be?" She sprung from her seat and stomped her little feet in outrage.

This time, the sigh escaped. Clara had only heard a fraction of what he said. It was clear she should have been a son and not a daughter, with these ideals. All he could do now was hope Miss Lewisham would be the one to tame his daughter.

"Clara, Clara, you, my child, are incorrigible."

She shrugged and picked up another sugar plum. It seemed that, as far as she was concerned, their conversation was finished. He picked up one of the sweet treats and plopped it into his mouth. The oversweet fruits exploded sickeningly on his tongue, and Clara giggled at his pinched face.

"Father, I think you are too old to eat sugar plums. Which I am glad for, as I do not like to share."

With that, she grabbed one more and walked confidently out of the room, leaving him shaking his head.

Chapter Five

"**I** have orders to show you to your rooms, Miss Lewisham."

Maribel followed the butler—Mr Jones, he had told her dryly when she had enquired—to the staircase and was then handed over to a maid. No names were given, and this time she did not ask, suspecting they had met one too many governesses to bother with introductions. The wooden balustrade was smooth under her fingertips as she glided her hand across it, using her other to hold up her skirts. She was so thrilled to be dressed in her new governess clothes that mother had made for her, and the muted colours did not dampen her excitement. Her mother was a talented seamstress, and without her, new clothing was impossible. The soft wool skirt made a satisfying swoosh when she walked, and paired with her freshly-polished half boots, she felt ready for any challenge

The maid led her down a long hallway, right to the very end.

My new room.

The maid held the door open for her, and she crossed the threshold and came face-to-face with a room more than double her own back home. The furnishings were rich—even with her half boots, she could feel the plush rug beneath her feet. A large four-poster bed tempted her to throw herself upon it like her younger brothers would have.

Decorum, Maribel.

An elegant desk was positioned against a large window framed by yellow drapes, and the natural sunlight poured in.

A beautiful space to review my lessons!

There were two dressers, a washstand, a long mirror, and a bed almost twice the size of her own back home. It was all so beautiful. So beautiful that it made her feel out of place. The room was fit for a lady, not a simple governess.

"I assume the room is to your liking, Miss Lewisham?"

"Yes, it is. Lovelier than I could have ever imagined."

"His grace wants you to be comfortable. He has requested one of the maids to attend you each day, and we will arrange a bath for you upon request."

Maribel found the information surprising. She had truly not expected to be treated with so much care. Perhaps the duke was not as cold as he had seemed.

"I can help you unpack."

"Can I do that later? I am eager to meet Lady Clara and spend some time with her before we start our lessons tomorrow."

Maribel was hoping to get some insight into her new charge and consider the best approach.

"I will check with Mr Jones and be back momentarily."

Taking this as her cue to begin the apparently very important unpacking, she opened her trunk and gave the maid a small smile. Maribel bit her lip and started to unpack her clothing, turning her back on the maid. She has been warned of this, that some of the staff would take a disliking to the station she now found herself in. She was not titled nor did she have any relation to anyone in the peerage. She was also not lower-class, born into a life of potential destitution and eager for any work. She was middle-class, genteel, and born to a family where she had had a privileged upbringing compared to many. Well-fed, educated, and clothed, Maribel knew she was lucky. Her own hands were soft and smooth, while a maid's were dry and rough from cleaning and caretaking. So, she understood why there was an instant hostility. But this did not mean Maribel had not hoped to make a friend.

"How long have you been in employment with His Grace?"

"Not very long."

"It is a very beautiful home to be working in—that is how I feel, anyway. I have never been in such a lovely home."

Moving to the dresser, she fingered the mahogany. The piece was clearly a Hepplewhite, and the rug beneath her feet was obviously another Aubusson. Even though she was hired help, her role as governess still allowed for certain privileges.

"If you say so. Cleaning is cleaning, no matter where you are. It is still dusty and dirty and leaves your hands raw."

Holding back a sigh of disappointment, Maribel realised she would need to admit defeat. On this occasion anyway.

A throat being cleared drew her attention to the doorway. Mr Jones was waiting for her.

"Lady Clara will see you now, Miss Lewisham."

Maribel felt her spark reignite at the thought of meeting her new charge. Eagerly, she followed the butler back down the winding hallway to another large room, this one filled with anything a young lady may want and need: a desk, a pianoforte, an easel, shelves full of books–it was incredible. And sitting in a large armchair that engulfed her small body was her charge. All fair curls and bright blue eyes, like a little cherub wearing a yellow day dress, she watched Maribel with narrowed eyes. Suspicion? Reproach?

I am very unpopular for the second time today, it seems.

"Miss Maribel Lewisham, may I present you to Lady Clara."

Maribel gave a small curtsey and beamed her biggest smile at the unhappy little girl.

"It is so wonderful to meet you, Lady Clara."

"I shall leave you both to your, ah, acquaintance." The butler spoke hastily and made himself scarce.

"This room is very resourceful. My mind is already racing with lessons and all the fun we will have."

"I hate lessons."

"You are yet to be part of one of my lessons, so you may very well change your opinion."

"My last governess thought the same. She left shortly after."

The little imp is trying to intimidate me, scare me off!

"The profession is not for everyone, I am afraid. I will not be deterred so easily."

Clara lifted her eyebrows but had no immediate retort, so she pressed on.

"Have you mastered the pianoforte?"

"No, my last two governesses did not play well themselves."

"Oh really?"

"Yes, I asked them to teach me a song, but they had to play it first, and it sounded terrible. I chuckled so very much."

"Is that so? I happen to be a very accomplished musician, so I will give my apology now that I will not be able to make you laugh at my efforts. But I can promise I will show you how to play."

Clara gave a small shrug, seemingly confused by Maribel.

"You do not look very old to be a governess, but you must be to.... "

"Clara, that is not a kind thing to say."

Any reprimand about manners that had been running

through Maribel's mind flew away as she turned to face the duke. Secretly, she applauded him for the firm scold. It surprised her that he would do so, seeing how dismissive he had been with her earlier. A little glimmer of respect for him sprung forth. He was clearly determined about the education of his daughter. Remembering her own manners, she gave a small smile and nod at his arrival.

"Your Grace."

"Miss Lewisham."

Chapter Six

Thomas had been admiring the way Maribel was handling his impertinent daughter. Clara was becoming more difficult by the day, and he had no idea what to do. When he'd last spoken to his close friend and confidante, the Duke of Lesterwich, at White's, the man had said the very sentence that all his other friends purposely avoided.

"What if you remarry, give her a mother figure?"

Thomas had shaken his head vehemently, insistently dismissing the suggestion. Marriage was not an option. He did not need a male heir—he had male relatives. He did not need another woman dependent on him. His first wife had died birthing the child he now had no control over. A mistress, an affair, or a skilled courtesan catered to his sexual urges, and emotional attachment was not an option. Well, at least to him. And those sexual urges were stirring at the idea of Maribel, which was terribly foolish, considering how much he needed her appointment to be successful. Returning to the situation at hand, he *tsk*'d aloud.

"Clara, that is not a kind thing to say," he scolded. It never ceased to amaze him that a child so sweet and innocent looking could wreak such havoc.

"Your Grace."

"Miss Lewisham."

"Father," Clara squealed, running over to him.

Catching her before she collided with his legs, he patted her absentmindedly on the head, his attention still on Maribel.

"What lessons do you have planned for the day? Music?"

"Yes, Your Grace, I would like to assess Lady Clara's pianoforte knowledge to determine where I should begin with my teachings. It is a fine instrument for any young lady to master."

He observed the encouraging smile she gave to Clara—it brightened her face with a soft warmth he found alluringly attractive. Realising his thoughts were again slipping in a dangerous direction, he threw her a dismissive look, wiping the smile from her face.

"I shall leave you both to your lesson."

Is there anything I can do for you, Your Grace?"

Mr Jones stood at attention, ready to attend to his every whim.

"A glass of claret while I write this letter to Lesterwich."

He had initially planned on heading into London to see his friend in person, but the arrival of Miss Lewisham now urged him to remain. However, being at the estate meant he had no friends to divulge his deepest thoughts to, so a letter would need to suffice. And there was no one he trusted more than his friend and fellow duke's.

Lesterwich,

I have chosen to write to you as I am not yet certain when I will return to London. I have acquired a new governess, and we now wait and see if my angelic child will drive her off in the upcoming days. Speaking of the governess, she is certainly a horse of another colour. She is quite unlike any governess I have ever met, and as you know, I have had my fair share. Her name is Miss Maribel Lewisham. She is young and hails from a nearby town with a middle-class upbringing. However, unlike the dowdy, sour, and plain women that have been coming in and out of employ, Maribel is honied sunshine. Her hair sheens vibrantly, a dark and rich brown. Her doe eyes are the colour of roasted chestnuts and equally as warm. Her skin is alabaster, as if she bathed in milk each night. And underneath her plain clothing is a body ripe with sensuous curves that beg to be caressed. I know what you must thinking—this fool is besotted. Fear not, I am only putting my thoughts to paper to rid the musings from my mind. A tryst with my daughter's new governess would only mean disaster, but the chit is tempting indeed. Her personality is haughty and indifferent, which captivates me. I am in a fit of rage at her *impertinence and equally bewitched by her nerve. I would like nothing more than to take my hand to her bare bottom and be the one who teaches her a lesson.*

By the time this letter reaches you, I will most likely be headed to London, as I shall know if the appointment is progressing without a hitch. And by that point, my loins will surely be at their bursting point and only will I find release without burden at some fair establishment of ill repute.

My letter is not all musings on my depraved thoughts, but my interest in the last venture you spoke of. I am happy to contribute 200 pounds to this mining expedition. You have made it sound promisingly profitable. I will arrange the funds to be delivered to you.

Until we meet next my friend, stay in good health and wealth.

T. Denby

Feeling slightly more relaxed about the impact his new employee was having on him, he sipped the rest of his claret slowly, savouring the depth of the berries and tannins as he pondered his next few days spent at the estate. There were ledgers to keep him busy, and he could indulge in a hunt. There was no need to be distracted by the governess. No need at all.

Chapter Seven

Maribel had decided to give lessons out in the gardens today. Maybe some fresh air and flora would improve Clara's mood. Their first day inside at the pianoforte had been challenging and tiresome. She had held her temper, which was sorely tested, more so than her impish younger brothers ever had. Clara had refused any simple instruction of the keys, instead jamming them with her hands and making a most dreadful ruckus. But Maribel knew the little girl was testing her. Waiting for her to break like all the governesses who had come before her. This knowledge only strengthened her resolve. She refused to be outwitted by a child.

They were sitting at a table in a garden filled with cheerful sunlight and well-manicured flowerbeds. Maribel read the myth of Pandora's box from Hesiod's "Works and Days" in an attempt to pique the child's interest.

"What do you think of it so far, Lady Clara?"

"She sounds very hasty and selfish."

Interesting that Clara recognised these traits, however, so clearly demonstrated them without repent.

"Indeed, but there is a lesson that can be learned here. Tempering curiosity, acting with caution and not haste. Heeding advice and *listening*."

She had seen Clara's eyes glaze over as she spoke, so she emphasised the word, hoping to regain her attention.

Instead, Clara got up and moved to the flower bed, pulling petals off the blooming hyacinths.

"You are ruining the flowers, My Lady, come back and sit down."

Clara ignored her, and Maribel looked down at the book to hide her frustration. To her surprise, when she looked up, Clara was back in her seat watching her expectantly. Maribel gave her a warm smile.

"Thank you, let us proceed. This time, I want you to read out the next verse." Maribel handed her the book.

Maribel took the opportunity to pick up her glass and have a drink and saw Clara watching her intently. Suddenly suspicious, Maribel held the drink out in front of her.

"Lady Clara, if I look in my cup, will I find something in there?"

"Yes, Miss Maribel, you will find the lemonade," she replied with feigned innocence.

Maribel was not fooled. These were the same signs her brothers displayed when they were playing one of their tricks. Bringing the glass to her face, she peered inside and gasped.

A bee! A. Dead. Bee.

"Lady Clara!"

The little imp laughed so heartily that she clutched her belly. It was evident she considered this trick to be full of hilarity.

"What would have happened, Lady Clara, if I had drunk from this glass and the bee became lodged in my throat?"

Clara stopped laughing and stared at her with wide eyes.

"If I had begun to choke, do you know how you could have provided me with aid?"

She shook her head with regret.

Finally, remorse!

"I had considered today's lesson out in the sun in the beautiful garden to be a treat, but you have shown yourself to be undeserving. I want you to return to the classroom and write an apology."

Maribel was expecting resistance and steadied herself to stay firm, but instead, the child nodded.

"I am very sorry, Miss Maribel. I did not even think of that."

Maribel knew she could easily say all was forgiven and comfort her, but then the lesson would not stick. She needed to be firm.

"You need to think about your actions. Actions have consequences."

Clara nodded obediently and made her way back to the manor. Pleased with the outcome, Maribel inwardly congratulated herself. She had even turned the lesson into a test to gauge Clara's writing skill.

Maribel watched Clara dutifully pen her note of apology with satisfaction. The feeling was marred by the interruption of His Grace, who wanted her to join him for the evening meal to discuss Clara's progress. Progress? It had been two days. And Clara had been horrid. Too distracted by his request, she ended her lesson with Clara and went to freshen up and use the quiet time to think of the evening ahead. It was endearing how he had peeped over Clara's shoulder and complimented her writing. It was evident that Clara was not accustomed to this attentiveness from her father, and she had revelled in the kind words he had spoken. The sweet moment had tugged at her heart, seeing the harsh man soften with fatherly attention.

Maribel ignored the voice inside her head that taunted her that this was the reason she was so concerned with her appearance—pinching her cheeks and tightening her stays to enhance her attractiveness. All the thoughts were going back and forth in her mind, like a buzzing bee darting in and out of the flower's centre in search of pollen. Bee. Her thoughts travelled to earlier, and the contrite apology letter penned by Clara. It was the first piece of work her young charge had produced where she had put in effort. The writing was legible and neatly spaced. There were a few minor spelling errors Maribel was already planning on using in their next lesson. Things finally seemed to be improving with Clara, but what about the duke? The man was maddening with the to-and-fro of mixed feelings he incited with his contradictory demeanour. Cold as a winter's morning frost one moment, and the next, warming her skin with a simple look as if she was naught but kindling.

She sat at her dresser and brushed her hair, dragging the brush in heavy strokes through her thick, brown tresses. Thomas—as she referred to him in her mind—had asked her to eat with him later this evening. The request had seemed casual, just an unassuming question as he had taken his leave. But this did not abate the underlying tension this man had aroused, as she recalled what it had felt like when she was last in his presence. It was the glint in his grey eyes and the tension in the air that surrounded them, like the humming of a bee you hear up close. The moment had reverberated, making it visceral. *Egad, back to the bee again!* She needed to stay calm, knowing he, too, would be baiting her. Maribel had not anticipated that she would be required to strategically navigate her charge *and* her employer like a Roman centurion leading a legion of men to war. Taking one last look at her appearance and giving her cheeks a final pinch, she decided she was ready to march.

Chapter Eight

The dining room was not usually a space of mirth. It could, at times, contain a steady stream of chatter or polite nonsense, but usually meals were silent and what he preferred. However, tonight was the first time he could recall where the silence—the absence of any words, just the clinking of cutlery—made him feel awkward. He—a duke, a man of standing, of import—was uncomfortable seated at his own dining table as a result of a simple governess. A simple governess whose honied voice he yearned to hear. Looking at her, he gave a small shake of his head.

The chit is anything but simple, he conceded begrudgingly.

Her manners were impeccable. Put the latest fashionable gown on her body, and she would be comparable with any lady of standing. The cream and brown of her ensemble on their own were dull, nondescript colours. On her body, he could not help but note the way the cream brought out the softness of her skin. The brown skirts drew warmth from her chestnut eyes. He was trying to eat, focusing on his next mouthful, but the tightening in his groin kept making him place his fork down. Her movements were dainty, her small bites chewed slowly, and for a moment, he wanted to laugh at how oblivious she was to the tension suffocating the room. Or so he thought.

"Is there a problem Your Grace?" she asked without looking at him.

"Problem?" he repeated, caught by surprise.

"Yes. A problem. You keep looking at me in the most peculiar way."

Damn her! But why does her besting me delight me at the same time?

"Is that so? And how would you know that I have been watching you? You have not turned my way, not once."

In response, she finally looked up and made eye contact. And she smiled. A wicked, seductive smile.

"Well now I know for certain, as you just confirmed it. Your Grace."

Termagant! It seemed she was determined to infuriate him! And the way she addressed him—she said the right words, *Your Grace*, but he noted the hint of disdain when she did so.

"Well played, Maribel. Savour the moment, as it is not often, if at all, that you will best me. And when we are alone, you can call me Thomas. See if my name can roll off your tongue with less disdain than when you address me by my standing."

Ahh, the hint of a rosy blush taints her creamy cheeks.

Momentarily mollified by the abrupt turn of events and having gained the upper hand, he kept talking.

"If you must know, I was admiring your table manners."

"I hope they meet expectation?"

"They do, I believe my daughter is in capable and well-cultured hands."

He had not meant for his voice to drop to a low octave that suggested flirtation. And for all her innocence, it was not lost on her, as her blush now burned claret red. He knew he was toying with her. She also knew it. There was a steely glint in her eye that belied her flushed face.

"Lady Clara has much potential in many areas if she applies herself." Her voice was calm as she tried to gain control of the conversation.

"Your daughter is very clever and has much imagination and energy, and my aim is to channel this potential into her lessons."

"Very good, Miss Lewisham, very good. I take it she has yet to scare you away then."

"I do not scare very easily, Your Grace."

She boldly met his gaze as she spoke, sending a veiled warning as he entwined his fingers under his chin and placed his elbows on the table.

"No, I can see you do not. I wonder why that is? Why you are so bold?"

She faltered under his intense gaze, unable to hold the eye contact any longer.

"As I informed you, I have younger twin brothers. They oft tried my patience with foolish pranks and wilful ignorance. But I am grateful for such, as they bolstered my fortitude."

"And you lived with your brothers and family in the town of Cheltenshire. What does your father do?"

"He and my uncle are linen drapers and share duties between their shops in Cheltenshire and London. My mother is also a skilled seamstress, whose tutelage I have benefited from."

As he had expected, a middle-class upbringing, but why a governess? She could have made a fine match with a young man in her class. Realising he could just ask her, making himself the bold one, he did. Her face flushed again as surprise opened her eyes wide.

"Why did you choose the solitary life of a governess and not a marriage and family of your own?"

She clearly found this line of questioning inappropriate, and the room was silent as he awaited her answer. Or perhaps she would not answer, as the silence grew.

"I love to learn, and I love to impart what I learn. When you become a wife, those opportunities diminish as your time is spent caring for others and a home. I had the benefit of choosing my path, and this is the one I chose."

Her words were so heartfelt that it gave him a pang of guilt for being so forthright this evening. All he had cared for was abating his own curiosity.

"I apologise, Miss Lewisham, if I have overstepped in any line of questioning tonight. I just found myself very curious."

To his surprise, she chuckled, bringing her dainty hand up to her mouth to mute the lilting sound.

"You find my apology amusing?" He raised his eyebrows in enquiry laced with amusement.

"No, no, Your Grace. It was your use of the word curiosity. I read to Lady Clara today the myth of Pandora's box, which, as you would know, is a tale that explores the follies of curiosity. Lady Clara, in her own words, found Pandora hasty and selfish."

"That does explain your mirth but now leads me to question whether your meaning is that I am hasty and selfish?" Her impertinence had escaped again, and this time, instead of feeling infuriated at her lack of respect for their class differences, he found himself aroused by her nerve.

"That was not my intent, I misspoke," she said hastily, realising her faux pas. He was about to respond, to continue their sparring of words, when she stood abruptly.

"It is getting late Your Grace, if you will please excuse me, I shall retire for the evening."

Disappointed that she was ending their exchanges of wits, he simply nodded.

Maybe I should have gone to London.

Chapter Nine

Maribel was breathing heavily by the time she reached the haven of her room. Was it due to her quick steps or the maddening company of the duke? The emotions he had stirred in her were almost unnatural—urges she had never felt before, only heard of. His voice had caressed her as if his hand had been stroking her. His gaze had made her pulse quicken, his broody grey eyes seeing straight through her soul. The desire that had pooled in her belly was as exciting as it was alarming, and the compulsion to place her hand between her legs was almost too hard to ignore. Even the tips of her breasts were enraged, her nipples hardened pebbles. Shaking her head and arms, Maribel tried to rid herself of these sensations. *Focus on how angry he made you,* she scolded herself!

The way he watched me like I was some succulent dish. The superior tone that constantly reminds me of our difference in class, no matter how well-mannered and cultured I may be. She shook her head, knowing it was not all quite true. He was genuinely attentive and curious about her. And she could not help but see his own indecision when responding to her. They were caught in a dance that had no choreography, no sheet music. Each step was on instinct, baited with emotion and reaction.

Slipping off her shoes, she began to pull at her skirts when there was a very faint knock at her door. She could not bring herself to ask who it was—she knew it was him.

"Maribel." The quiet demand was clear through the wooden barricade separating them.

She opened the door and looked up at him, attempting to keep composed, not wanting to give him any satisfaction.

"Did you forget to tell me something, Your Grace?"

He rested his hand on the doorway, shifting his weight as he looked down to meet her gaze.

"I did, Miss Lewisham. This."

He bent his head and captured her mouth hotly. No person had ever pressed their mouth against her own, and the duke's full lips covered hers like a well-fitted glove. Instinctively, she closed her eyes. and flashing lights sparked against her eyelids as he let her lips go before taking them again, more roughly this time.

He placed his hands at her waist and pulled her close, so her curves now pressed against the hard expanse of his body. His mouth captured and released her own with a skill that was controlled and reckless all at once.

"We mustn't, Your Grace," she murmured, but made no attempt to move away.

The space between her legs was now throbbing, and it was not her own hand she had the urge to place there, but his. Without realising, she had begun to grind her pelvis against his. He moaned and swore against her mouth, lifting her up slightly so she could feel the hardness between his legs. Her hands, which had been limp at her side, now held his arms for balance as his kiss deepened. His tongue was in her mouth, again duelling with her—this time not with words, but with deft strokes that were setting her body aflame. Abruptly, she felt him pull away, holding her at arm's length as they both panted wildly, trying to regain their breath.

"Miss Lewisham, I am so very sorry." He may have said the words, but he did not look sorry. He looked frenzied, his grey eyes a raging tempest as he gripped her arms tightly.

"I think I should retire, Your Grace." Her voice was faint, all that she could muster amid the confusion of this unexpected and fierce exchange. He let go of her arms but did not speak, still staring at her with a wild look in his eyes, and while it excited her more than scared her, common sense made her spin on her heel and close the door. Quickly changing, she got into bed and pulled the blankets over her head so she could relive what had just happened. She found she was trembling as the effervescence slowly left her body. She had oft wondered what it would be like to be kissed. Never in a thousand years would she have thought her first kiss would be with a duke—a man that was equal parts infuriating and enticing. His kiss had left a burning imprint on her still tingling lips. His tongue had been inside her mouth, and her own inside his. She sucked on one of her own fingers. The sensations that had erupted deep in her loins were the most pleasant of all surprises, and she cupped herself with her other hand, feeling the pulsing of her femininity. Her heartbeat was slowing down to a normal pace, and she laid her hands on the bed. Sleep was eluding her, but she knew it would come as she allowed the replay of what had transpired to wash over her again. She would fall asleep, yes, but her last thoughts before sleep took her would certainly be of Thomas's lips.

Chapter Ten

Thomas stocked back and forth in his rooms, nude and frustrated. That innocent exchange with Maribel had been one of the most erotic encounters he had experienced. No courtesan had ever elicited such raw passion. Perhaps what had made it so delicious was that it was so wrong. She was young and innocent and should be completely out of reach as his child's governess. Unless...he employed her instead as his mistress? He was disgusted at the depraved idea. Miss Lewisham was a fine governess and what his child needed.

Tomorrow, I will go to London. Put distance between myself and her siren song, because that's what it is. I am drawn to her like a mariner passing his ship in the night, tempted by the call of an ethereal being that would only mean my destruction.

"Mr Jones," he bellowed, "have my trunks packed. I head to London tomorrow."

He was rock-hard, and he knew it would not go away, not without release. A release he would now need to give himself, he thought with a scowl. He could not and should not lie with Maribel. Their kiss had been bad enough. He moved to his bathing room, where a freshly-drawn tub beckoned him to sink into its warm depths. *If only I was sinking into the warm depth between Maribel's legs.* He released all his lewd thoughts as the hot water eased his tension. Thomas did not care to tend to his own releases, and it had rarely been an issue as he spent his time with many women who would. What happened tonight would not rest until he allowed himself to sink into it. The warm water sluiced off his body as he tried to find a comfortable position from which to hang his head over the edge. His erection had not gone down, and he was powerless to make it do so. Only his hand would be of use to him, like a green boy who cannot find a woman to touch him. Taking himself in hand, he began to stroke himself firmly as he replayed the lust Maribel had exhibited. Her siren call that had made him kiss her like a man starving. The feel of her hips pressed against him, needing something that she had no idea of. He started to stroke himself faster and more firmly. Her innocence proved to be a heady aphrodisiac as he pictured those doe eyes wide in surprise as he made her feel new plea-sure after pleasure. He moved his hand more quickly, the water splashing about as he strained to finish. He roared his release, letting the sexual tension she had wound up in him erupt into a moment of bliss.

"Damn her!" he yelled to the empty room, the moment soon gone as he began to fixate on her. He needed distance, distraction. He needed to be away from her.

Thomas tapped his foot impatiently as his postillions prepared to mount their horses. He had chosen his chariot for the trip to London because he wanted the room to loll about and brood. And drink. He had made sure the chariot was stocked with bottles of claret ready to be drunk. Thomas had elected to not say goodbye to Clara lest he encounter that damnable Miss Lewisham, and he felt a slight pang of guilt towards his daughter. This thought seemingly conjured the child as shouts of "Father, Father!" moved towards him. Turning, he noted that Maribel walked behind her. Her face was devoid of smile and her eyes were slightly narrowed, so it seemed she had also planned on avoiding him today.

"Father, how could you leave me and not say goodbye?" Clara cried.

"I am sorry, darling, I simply did not want to make a fuss. I will not be gone long."

"Gone where?" Her bottom lip dropped dangerously low.

"London, and I promise I will bring you back some marzipan."

"And a new dress and bonnet." The smile was back on her face—the act of negotiation in her favour always defused an oncoming tantrum.

"I shall, my darling." He bent down to kiss her cheek.

Satisfied, Clara ran back towards the manor, leaving Maribel standing there with strong disapproval etched on her face.

"Is there something the matter, Miss Lewisham?" he asked, trying to keep his tone bored.

"Yes, there is. I do not think it is wise to reward outbursts or bargaining with promises of gifts. This leads to disobedience."

"Miss Lewisham, I shall remind you that I have hired you to govern my daughter, not myself, so please refrain from teaching me lessons."

Her cheeks flamed, and she opened her mouth as he braced himself to be lashed with her tongue.

"You are correct, Your Grace, and I do apologise. I am but

a lowly governess." She spoke coolly to his surprise. They stared at each other for a moment, and she broke contact first, walking away without a word. Thomas stepped inside his carriage and took a seat, pondering her words.

A lowly governess? But she is just a governess? Am I to feel bad for this or be the one to blame? Such impertinence—why do I find it so attractive? He realised it hurt him that she would say such words. In his unkindness, what else would she think? It was clear to him this trip to London would be filled with the maddening chatter of his own psyche.

Chapter Eleven

Maribel stared out the window at the sky—which had brightened her day with sunlight and warmth yesterday—that was now melancholy, the shade of ash at the bottom of a fireplace.

Melancholy to match my mood and the deep unease that has settled inside me.

The duke—she would no longer think of him as Thomas—had kissed her fervently, like a man starved of thirst, only to bid her adieu as if she was the lowliest of his employees.

What treatment did I expect after resorting to such wantonness?

Cursing herself, she replayed the lustful exchange and was unable to prevent the flipping sensation in her stomach. Maribel could not deny she had willingly received his affection, nor could she deny that she had enjoyed it. She was left to wonder whether mere moments of bliss were worth everlasting regret?

"Miss Lewisham, did you hear what I asked? What am I to do next?"

Shaking herself, she turned to Clara, who sat beside her on

the pianoforte chair. The child was watching her impatiently, awaiting her next instruction. Which was a welcome surprise. The events of yesterday must still resonate, as Lady Clara had been obedient and in a positive spirit, even suggesting Maribel begin her pianoforte lessons. Thankfully, Clara—who had played her a song as soon as they sat down—had an ear for music and a natural talent, one Maribel did not possess but could surely teach. Music fell on her ears without eliciting joy or displeasure. It was just sound, sound that could register as good or bad.

"I am sorry, My Lady, you will have my full attention. I want to understand your knowledge further. Press each key starting with A working to G, and between each stroke, I want you to wait a few moments to just allow the sound to wash to over you."

Nodding, Clara began right away, and Maribel could not help but feel pride at the obedience she demonstrated.

Her father has not the faintest idea about how best to raise this young lady.

The thought of Thomas made her jaw tense. He insulted her. He kissed her. He admonished her.

Blazes! Why can I still feel his lips upon my own? Was I branded?

Maribel was prepared to admonish herself for such a missish thought, but the loud clanging of the pianoforte broke through her rumination.

"How sweet, Miss Lewisham, it is a kitty!" squealed Clara.

Maribel glared at Mr Whiskers. He should know better than to demonstrate such impolite behaviour! He returned her glare with a sniff and moved his attention to Clara, who was happily patting the length of his back, telling him how sweet he was. He purred with satisfaction and hopped onto Clara's lap and curled up.

"Can we keep it? What shall we call it? How do we know

if it is a boy or girl?" Clara peppered her with these questions, not taking a breath. Her excitement was palpable, and Maribel withheld a sigh. Mr Whiskers had captured her heart, and this was a side to Clara she had not yet seen. Sweet and caring.

"I think he is a boy, so why don't we call him Mr Whiskers? See how they are very long?"

"Yes, they are, and that is a dimber name! And look, you can tell he likes it! Don't you, Mr Whiskers?" Clara crooned to the preening cat.

"On the topic of keeping Mr Whiskers, your father, I believe, does not enjoy a cat for a pet."

"He will if I say I want to keep him," Clara replied smugly.

This time, Maribel let the sigh escape. No doubt she was right, but that was beside the point. She was determined to make Clara less brazen—it was unbecoming.

"I shall think on it. Now, enough hum and haw! Let's return to your lesson. Place Mr Whiskers on the ground."

Maribel eyed him to ensure he obeyed, and despite a reproachful glare, he curled up under the chair.

"Now, Lady Clara, let us begin again with hearing to the sound of each key."

Chapter Twelve

T homas stalked the length of the Duke of Lesterwich's drawing room. He had called upon his friend as soon as he had arrived in London. The time was 3:00 p.m., and his friend, of course, was still retired, no doubt having had a rambunctious evening. He threw back the glass of port and poured himself another, since even Lesterwich's staff had noted his black mood and scurried out of sight instead of waiting on him. They were a discreet and loyal staff, compensated handsomely to stay silent about His Grace's activities. That courtesy extended to His Grace's friends, and Thomas had spent many an evening of debauchery at this home.

This is no time to reminisce, it is my own impulsive depravity that has landed me in this predicament!

Thomas could not recall a prior period where he had spent this much time berating himself. In fact, he rarely saw any error in his ways. Maribel's hurt expression appeared before him, and he felt his lip curl into a scowl. He could not decide if he was angrier at her innocent inexperience or at himself for feeling a flicker of guilt, for once.

"She is naught but a governess!" he spat out, throwing himself down on a winged chair, exasperated with himself.

"Ahh, the governess. She must be more than just a simple governess." Marcus, the Duke of Lesterwich, stood in the doorway smiling. And in his hand was a letter.

"I see my correspondence arrived before I did."

"Indeed, it did. So, you forgive me for not being here to welcome you as soon as you arrived, but I gathered you would still be pining in the country for this decadent-sounding *governess*."

Marcus took a seat opposite him, spinning the letter through his fingers, clearly amused by the sight of his friend.

"I am glad you are taking such joy in my misfortune."

"I do not take joy in your misfortune. It is more a gleeful satisfaction to see and read you—" Marcus shook the letter at him "—so muddled. And by a woman, no less. Nay, and by a governess."

Gritting his teeth and clenching his fists, he shook one menacingly at his friend, who simply laughed.

"I will stop nettling you despite the joy it is giving me, lest we resort to fisticuffs." Marcus held his hands up in mock surrender, clearly still amused.

"Marcus, I am at a loss. Over a woman? Can you believe it?" Marcus was not only one of his closest friends, but a fellow member of the Wayward Duke Alliance, an alliance of dukes who could confide in and rely on one another. This issue he was facing was an embarrassing one, and he would prefer it not be made public. For all Marcus's nettling, he knew he could trust the man to say nothing.

"It is quite strange. I must admit your attitude towards woman is generally one of contempt. You take your pleasure and then take your leave. I cannot recall you ever wooing and courting a woman."

"That is exactly right! Not even with women more suitable to my station!"

"You know, you sound every bit the wiseacre when you speak this way?" Marcus asked with raised brows. His friend wore his red hair long, so for a moment, they disappeared.

"That is not my intent—it is simply fact," he retorted stubbornly.

"Let me ask you this, have you made these 'facts' known to Miss Lewisham?"

"I may have." The impact of his actions dawned on him. *Am I really that rude and insensitive? Yes.*

"That is simply who I am, though. And I have never cared before how it may come across?" He asked himself and Marcus the question, hoping that, between the two of them, they would solve this problem.

"I think you have genuine emotion for her. Something you have not felt in a long time, if ever."

"I have barely known her a sennight!" He shook his head at his friend.

"I do not think that matters. Emotions cannot always be explained—they are not logical. They are feelings."

"When did you become such a goosecap?"

Marcus laughed.

"I have always been more mature in the ways of the heart. That's why I have so many long-term female acquaintances that I can call upon at any time. You, on the other hand, become easily bored and easily insensitive due to your lack of care."

"Some friend you are," he said gruffly. "Well, Marcus, since you are the one with all the answers, what should I do?"

"I think you need to apologise. And then I think you need to decide what it is you want and be honest and expect to be rejected. You may want a tryst, while she may not. What I do know from your letter is that you are besotted with her. And if you want her to continue in your employ, you need to determine how far you want to pursue the matter."

Thomas knew his friend spoke true, and begrudgingly, he nodded.

"I will return home on the morrow. For now, let us get top-heavy."

Chapter Thirteen

Maribel marvelled that almost a sennight had passed without incident, but she was becoming suspicious at her young charge's oddly obedient behaviour in all things—even lessons she did not like, such as arithmetic. And it appeared to have something do with Mr Whiskers. All Maribel had to do was threaten to remove Mr Whiskers from their presence, and any unruliness Clara was beginning to display ceased in an instant. The more Maribel observed Clara's fascination with her cat, the clearer it became that Clara was a very misunderstood, very lonely little girl. The friendship and comfort she sought from Mr Whiskers was endearing, and the two had become inseparable. As a result, the rest of the household was now well aware there was a cat living with them. They had all noticed the same change in Clara, so everyone was prepared to plead ignorance to Mr Whiskers's presence.

Maribel eyed Clara, who was working on her arithmetic in deep concentration. Her smooth brow furrowed as she tried to get the right answer to earn time playing with Mr Whiskers.

"Do you need any help, Lady Clara?" Maribel asked gently.

"No, thank you, Miss Mari. I was paying attention during our lesson, and I will find the answer."

Proud of her fortitude, Maribel gave her an approving nod. Clara calling her Miss Mari was another positive sign of their progression, as it signified a personal affection. And she sorely missed her brothers calling her Mari.

It was going to be a shame when Thomas returned, and she had not yet decided how to navigate the situation with Mr Whiskers. Or their kiss. She had certainly decided that there would be no more kisses. His kisses were not worth jeopardising her employ.

Liar, a small voice inside her head whispered as she remembered the feel of his kiss. She knew it was foolish, since she was coming to very much enjoy being a governess. It was her calling! Maribel was feeling a little homesick for her mother and brothers and hoped His Grace would be so kind as to let her take time to visit. She was only a governess after all, her family all she had. While she was well aware of their class difference, it hurt when he said it. It took all her pride in her achievements away. And it infuriated her that she allowed the conceited man to have that power over her.

He has the power over my wages, not my mind.

"Miss Mari, here are my answers." Clara approached her with the paper she had been working on.

Ah, she had been paying attention, she said to herself, confirming Clara had arrived at the correct answer.

What a clever child indeed!

"Where did this cat come from?"

Chapter Fourteen

"**W**here did this cat come from?"

"Father, you are home!" Clara squealed, dropping the black feline on the floor and running towards him with outstretched arms.

"Yes, yes, I am home." He patted her fair head absent-mindedly. "And I ask again. why is there a cat in my home?"

Thomas swallowed a gasp of surprise when the cat met his stare and appeared to glower back at him.

Impertinence!

"Please father, this is Mr Whiskers. He is my new friend, isn't he, Miss Mari?"

He followed Clara's gaze to Maribel, who was standing stiffly in the middle of the room. Acknowledging his attention, she gave a simple curtsey.

"Your Grace."

"Why is my daughter's new friend covered in fur and walking on four legs? And since when do we refer to you as Miss Mari."

"Your daughter's new friend is covered in fur and uses four legs to roam because he is a cat. And 'we' do not need refer to me as Miss Mari, but Lady Clara can. It is a simpler and more comfortable form of address, given the time we spend in each other's company."

It was evident his absence had not made Maribel grow fonder. If anything, she seemed more aloof. He watched as she folded her arms in front of her, a defiant position which brought a smile to his face. She was not aloof but angry and trying to mask it with an air of indifference. He was not fooled, and he felt sweet gratification knowing he was not the only one who had been tormented by their exchange.

"Clara, can you please leave Miss Mari and I?"

"Only if Mr Whiskers can come with me."

His child, always the negotiator.

"Yes, take the wretched ball of fur and get it out of my sight. I will attend to it after I speak with Miss Mari."

Oblivious to the veiled threat, Clara squealed and scooped up Mr Whiskers, running from the room.

"Remember, Lady Clara, it is not proper for a lady to run," Maribel called after her.

"Forget being Miss Mari for a moment. Just be Maribel." He had not intended for his voice to lower as he moved towards her. He was now a predator stalking his prey, watching her chestnut eyes widen in alarm as he stopped in front of her. They were standing so close that he could see the pulse in her neck beating wildly as he invaded her personal space.

"And what is it you want, Your Grace?" she mustered while holding his gaze.

"Initially, I had returned from London intent on clearing up any misunderstanding about what occurred between us. Then I was met with the unwelcome surprise of cat in my home. And if I recall correctly, you had asked if you could keep a cat, and I had said no. Now that we are alone—no child, no cat, just you before me—I have no idea what to say, except that I am feeling the urge to kiss you again."

Maribel's jaw dropped at his frankness, and she took a step backwards.

"There is nothing to clear up, let us simply forget. And yes, the cat is mine, but as you can see, it has had a most welcome influence on Lady Clara—I have had days of productive lessons with Mr Whiskers in attendance. Lastly, that would be a very poor idea, Your Grace. You are my employer, and I your employee, just a governess if you recall. And as you well know, our classes do not mix, and they especially do not kiss."

With each sentence, her voice became more self-assured. That defiance had returned, and it was frustratingly attractive.

"If I was to ignore all we have just spoken and kiss you, what would you do?" He asked silkily.

Her face flushed crimson at his bold question. She did not answer with words, but he saw other signs of response. Her chestnut eyes warmed to a fire-roasted shade, the darkening irises parading her desire. Her small pink tongue darted out to moisten her lips. She did not say yes, but she did not say no, and perhaps she truly did not know. Her body, on the other hand, was screaming yes, and that was all he needed to know. Bending down to capture her lips, he was met by a hand.

"Your Grace, this is not about what I will or will not enjoy. It is about propriety. You are my employer and a duke, and I am responsible for your child's education. I think it is best if we hold each other at arm's length."

Thomas was speechless. She had turned him on his head again. On his journey home, that was the exact thing he had decided. And he had intended to offer an apology. Once he was in her presence, however, he had lost all his good sense! Frustrated that it had come from her, but remembering he had wanted to apologise, he reined in his temper.

"You are completely right, Miss Lewisham, and I would like to take this opportunity to offer my most heartfelt apology for how I have spoken to you. It has come to my attention that I have perhaps caused offence at our difference in...ah...class, and while it is a fact, I certainly do not look down on you."

She might have looked less stunned if he had slapped her.

Blazes, Is it so shocking that I could admit fault? Am I that rude?

"Thank you, Your Grace, that was most unexpected but most welcome."

"I am also many years your senior, and it is unbecoming how I have behaved."

"Our difference in age does not concern me, it is our difference in station."

Nodding at her, he tugged on his cravat not sure what to say next. With that direct frankness he had come to adore was a truth that weighed heavy as an anvil. Then it hit him—the cat! The change in topic he sorely needed.

"Now, what is the business with this cat?".

Chapter Fifteen

Maribel—still recovering from the duke's completely changed attitude—tried to remember her plan for explaining Mr Whiskers' presence. She would need to ponder the rest of their exchange when she was alone.

"It is I who now owes you an apology. The cat is mine—I had brought him with me, as I had not anticipated any reason you would say no. And when you did, it was not as if I could return home, so I thought I could wait till I visited my family."

He nodded and thankfully did not look to angry. Her relief turned to errant impulse, wanting to reach up and caress the grey streak in his dark locks.

"That explains that, but why is my daughter now enamoured with this cat?"

"His name is Mr Whiskers. It was not planned that they meet, he just appeared one lesson and Lady Clara was instantly besotted. And I must say, she has been so well-behaved during your time away. And in part, I think it is to do with Mr Whiskers. If she wants to play with him, she must participate and finish her lesson, which she has been doing without complaint. And overall, her persona has lifted happily, and I often see her smiling and hear her laughing joyously."

Maribel knew she had spoken quickly, barely taking a breath, and she hoped he had heard, as she surely would not remember it. His stormy eyes were fixed on her own, and it was making it hard for her to focus.

"A cat did all this. Really?" he asked as he stroked his chin thoughtfully.

"Mr Whiskers did, yes."

"He will remain the cat to me," he said drily, "though I must say, this change in my daughter is most welcome. I have been waiting for you to announce your resignation, as all the governesses did before you. But it seems you are no ordinary governess."

This time, she heard no insult but instead a compliment, and she felt her body flush.

"Thank you, Your Grace. That is very kind to say."

"Seems you are teaching me something after all, Miss Lewisham".

Giving her a slight bow, he left her standing there without another word, and she leaned back on the table, her legs weak from their exchange. Deciding it best she return to her room, she made haste for the privacy of her sanctuary.

Reaching her room, she kicked off her shoes, threw herself face down on the bed, and let out a muffled scream.

His complete change in behaviour and the apology had undone her resolve. This side of him was terribly attractive, and if he was to try and kiss her now, she would not hold him back with her hand. Instead, her hand would claw at his shirt and pull him closer. And it was such a foolish thing to be thinking. No matter how kind he was, it would never be possible to bridge the gap between their classes. Kisses with a man should lead to marriage, and the idea that she would marry a duke was inconceivable. Before meeting him, she had had no idea or need to marry or kiss anyone.

A knock interrupted her thoughts, and she asked who it was. It was one of the maids, so she opened the door.

"His Grace asked that you share the evening meal with him, as he would like to hear more about the sennight you spent with Lady Clara."

Nodding her understanding, she quickly closed the door before the maid could notice any other reaction. The last time they dined together had ended poorly and then had been followed with a kiss. Their earlier conversation suggested it would not repeat, but that thought caused a pang of angst. She wanted to feel that passion, but alas, it would need to remain unspoken.

Reminding herself to be unselfish and that this was about Clara, she freshened herself up and considered what insights she would share with him. There were many to choose from. Clara was reading and writing, and her skill with the pianoforte was improving.

Chapter Sixteen

Thomas had a strange sensation in his stomach that he had never experienced. It was all in a tremble as if he had swallowed a horde of butterflies and hundreds of little wings were beating inside of him.

By Jove, am I nervous?

Grunting in annoyance, he tugged at his cravat, suddenly stifled. All he was asking of her was to share a meal where she could regale him with his daughter's progress. Or so he kept telling himself. His journey home had given him considerable time to mull over the predicament of Maribel Lewisham. As a governess, she was doing well—remarkably well when he compared her to the previous employees. His return home had given him the welcome sight of Clara responding, behaving, and most importantly, learning! His pondering had led him to the conclusion that Maribel, delectable as she was, was simply a woman. And bedding her was not worth losing the first governess that was actually meeting the task. Knowing his rationale was sound, he had decided to keep Maribel at arm's length. All of that logic had escaped him as soon as he found himself back in her proximity. Her honeysuckle scent had been an aphrodisiac upon his senses. And she had not the faintest idea what she was doing to him.

"Miss Lewisham, please, sit," he said with a cordial sweep of his arm. She nodded with a smile, but he could sense she was nervous. Her eyes were wide, and she was biting her lower lip. Wanting to put her at ease, he turned the conversation immediately to Clara, waving his hand at the chestnut soup laid out before them.

"I have observed positive changes in Clara's behaviours and demeanour. How did you manage to do so much in such little time?"

He watched her bring a spoonful of soup to her mouth, her tongue furtively escaping her luscious mouth to lick the moisture that stained her lip. She swallowed and placed the spoon back down, her stare almost curious, watchful.

"Lady Clara is a very clever child. These behaviours, as you call them, were not who she was, but a manifestation of loneliness and a deep yearning for your attention."

His spoon froze on its way to his mouth at her brazen accusation that he did not give his daughter attention. A niggling voice in the back of his head whispered that his offence at her comment was because it held truth. Again, the impertinence with which she spoke to him astounded him, but he could not help but admire it. It had been a long time, if ever, since anyone dared to challenge him. Scooping up the woody-scented soup, he weighed his response while he ate, watching her watch him. Her eyes had slightly narrowed, and her posture was tense, waiting for him to reprimand her. This made him smile.

"You speak truth, I will not deny it. First, let me say I love my daughter. I will admit that I perhaps have not been the most attentive father. It seems you have taught me that, because before you, the thought had never occurred to me."

It was true—as he spoke the words out loud, an awareness

washed over him that it was he who had allowed his child to become so unruly.

"I am surprised you so readily agree to my observations. And that you admit that I, a simple governess, have been able to teach you something of value."

The impertinent chit did not even try to hide her smug smile of satisfaction, and he rolled his eyes in mock annoyance.

"So, not only have I created a child who exhibits such poor behaviour, but now a governess with hubris?"

Maribel blushed but held his gaze.

"And I now have a cat living under my roof—I really do not like cats, Miss Lewisham."

"If it helps, my plan had been to keep Mr Whiskers hidden from sight, especially yours."

"And now I have no choice except to allow this cat, this Mr Whiskers, to live in my home. Clara would never forgive me if I expelled the four-legged wretch."

Maribel broke out in a fit of giggles just as a servant brought in the next dish, his eyebrows rising in surprise at the intimate encounter. Thomas gave him a stern look, and he quickly laid down the food and left.

"Can you share with me what you find so amusing?"

"Your disdain for Mr Whiskers! What prejudice do you hold against cats?"

"Their attitudes. They lack obedience and humility, and the way they make eye contact, with such impertinence. It raises my ire."

"Yes, cats are full of unapologetic confidence—which is personally what I adore! Though I now understand why you react in such a way to Mr Whiskers. You are unyielding when it comes to your views, your needs, and your wants, and luckily for you, you can be."

Maribel lowered her head to daintily sniff the steamed mackerel emitting the scent of fennel and mint and smiled.

"This smells divine."

"You are right, Maribel. I am unyielding. My wants, my needs. And what I need and want right now—is you."

Chapter Seventeen

Maribel's breath caught in her throat, and the satisfied look in Thomas's eye told her he had heard the hitch. The room was silent except for the sound of her own blood pulsating through her body. It seemed to echo, almost deafening, as her desire overcame her. He stood and moved towards her. It was only a few steps, and she had no time to form a coherent thought.

"Maribel," he whispered gruffly, crooking his finger at her, "stand up and follow me.".

She stood and moved towards him, obeying the demand as he led her inevitably to his bedroom. The sensible, educated lady in her was telling her to stop and walk the other way. But Maribel did not want to hear that voice. She wanted to be reckless and foolish and feel passion that might otherwise be never known to.

They crossed the threshold and stood face to face, the top of her head came to his chin, and she looked up to meet eyes darkened with lust. He reached to cup her cheeks—the pressure gentle but firm as he held her jaw.

"I am tired of keeping distance between us. Pretending

there is not this inferno burning between us. I need to kiss you, to touch you. I need to be inside you, Maribel."

His voice was ragged as his words crashed down on her like heavy raindrops, titillating her senses. Instinctively, she rose to her toes as he lowered his mouth to capture her lips. This kiss was different from the previous ones shared. The pressure was deep and full of intention as he explored each pillow, pushing them apart so his tongue now controlled every pleasured nerve in her body. Her pulse was racing, at the base of her neck, in her chest, and at the core between her legs. Maribel threw her arms around his neck, not only to steady herself, but to surrender all that she was to him. A throaty growl escaped him at her acquiescence. Thomas scooped her up and carried her to the rug by the fire, gently placing her down.

He began to undress, the light of the flame revealing his muscular chest, dusted with hair that unleashed a primal urge to run her hands through it.

"Undress yourself, Maribel. I want you naked and laying back on that rug." She instantly obeyed at the dominance in his tone and began to unbutton her shirt, her fingers fumbling at the buttons. He watched her as he continued with slipping off his shoes and removing his pants.

In this moment, Maribel lost any decorum she had prided herself in as she cast her gaze straight to his manhood. It was hard and upright and, in its own way, a thing of natural beauty. She marvelled at the form. Maribel wanted to touch it, and Thomas was standing there with his legs parted, his devilish smile inviting her to follow her instinct.

"You are one with the devil tonight, Thomas. You are making me wanton."

Unsure of what to do, she crawled over so she was on her knees in front of him and stroked his manhood gently before taking it in hand. It was thick and soft, firm and hard, and it made no real sense except that, in all its glory, it was magnificent. Emboldened, Maribel ran her hands up and down the shaft, rubbing more firmly when she heard him moan, and tasting him with her tongue, which made him swear.

"Enough playing and teasing, Maribel. I want you to get back down on the carpet, on your back."

Part of Maribel was slightly insulted at the subservient position she was to assume, but the rest of her was still excited. Thomas sat down beside her and began to run his hands all over her body while he captured her lips in a soul-shattering kiss. He stroked his tongue against her own with such sensuality that moisture began pooling between her legs. Like he had read her mind, his fingers moved to her aching core, the strokes of his tongue and fingers now in unison. Her body was a bundle of nerves, and they all screamed for pleasure. Thomas laid back and pulled Maribel atop of him so she straddled him, giving him a full view of her upper body. Maribel tried to cover her breasts, but he held her hands apart.

"Do not hide yourself from me, Maribel. Your breasts are big and beautiful, and your nipples—I love the honey-hued areolas surrounding them."

He was massaging them as he complimented her, and her nipples were rock-hard under the praise. Maribel was becoming restless with all the sweet torture, and she knew Thomas was enjoying every moment of control he had over her.

"Maribel, do you want me to suck your nipples?

"Yes, Your Grace—no, no, Thomas, Your Grace—"

"Yes, Thomas, I want you to suck my nipples," he coached her.

She was frustrated by her weakness and the loss of the power. She wanted to be ravished by him, and she quickly echoed his words.

Thomas filled his hands with her breasts and sighed.

"They are perfect, Maribel, a perfect pair," he told her in a lazy drawl.

She tried to respond, but only a gasp escaped her mouth at the exquisite sensation of her nipple being sucked on. She moaned deeply and rolled her head from side to side. Thomas suckled and, to her pleasant surprise, bit them into such a frenzy she felt her own wet arousal dripping down her legs. Being of the one mind, he began to trail his hand up towards her center, which was now desperate for his attention.

"Maribel, you are so wet and ready for me."

He slipped his fingers inside of her, stroking her core intently. He flipped her onto her back. She was moaning and writhing on the carpet, clutching her own breasts, her head moving side to side. Thomas moved down her body and added his mouth to his fingers, sucking at her core, finding the sweet spot that held all the pleasure. Within moments, she exploded. Maribel could think of no other way to describe the intensity of the gratification spreading throughout her body.

"Are you certain you want me to claim you, Maribel?" he asked, but his eyes pleaded with her to say yes.

"Yes, Thomas, take me, I am yours."

She felt him enter her body, but the moment of him breaching her innocence did not cause pain as she had always been led to believe it would. And then she forgot all words. All that mattered was the rhythmic thrusting. Being flesh to flesh. Breathing in each other's breath. Until she shattered again, but this time, he shattered with her, and in that moment, it was all that mattered. She was his, and he was hers. No society walls between them. Only devoted passion.

Chapter Eighteen

Thomas could watch Maribel for hours. She had stirred something undiscovered inside him. An affection so tender and sweet, he had no inkling it existed. Certainly, no other woman had stirred such a feeling. His wife had stirred duty, a mistress desire. This soft and warm sensation spreading throughout him, especially in his chest, was most peculiar indeed and not unwelcome.

"You have the face of an angel when you sleep. Only when your eyes are open is it possible to see the impish woman I now so intimately know."

Thomas loved that he had her nude in his bed, because he was able to see the blush that spread from her cheeks down to the swell of her luscious breasts. The supple curves that he had known were hiding under her modest garb were more ample than he could have hoped. He stroked her thighs. Thighs that had gripped him with fervent passion. Thomas did not regret that he had taken her maidenhead. He had suspected she was a virgin, and if he was honest with himself, the fact had pleased him immensely. The primal male instinct to claim a woman and be the only man to have done so had always eluded him, it was just a given in marriage. Now, he knew what it meant and that only he had entered her most sacred place. The place that made her every inch a woman.

He felt her stiffen at the comment, and he cuddled her close, shushing her gently.

"I mean no offence, Maribel" he murmured, placing a gentle kiss on her shoulder.

"I know, and I am not offended. It just dawned on me that I am no longer a virgin."

"How does that make you feel?"

"Strangely, I feel like a woman. Which I always have been. Now that I know the touch of a man, it certainly feels different. Like I have somehow blossomed."

"Blossomed you have. Indeed, I felt you come alive in my arms, Maribel. It was a breathtaking experience—one I can truly say I have not experienced before."

Maribel lifted her head to meet his eyes, her face bright with questions.

"Forgive me for my boldness, but it is no secret that you have been with many women in this way. Thomas," she added with a smile.

He smiled back at his name on her lips.

"This is true, I have had many a bed-warmer. What is different is the emotion behind it. Maribel, you have burrowed under my skin like no other."

"What of Clara's mother?" she pressed, leaning her cheek on her hand while her other drew circles on his chest. Her eyes were intent as awaited his answer.

"The mother of my child—I came to care for her deeply. She was my wife. of course. It was no love match, more convenience. I was at an age to try for an heir, she was from a family of great title and wealth, and she was fair. I did come to adore her, to care for her, and I was bereft when she passed. I cannot profess I had fallen deeply in love or lust with her. The thing with emotion, Maribel, is that, until you experience the maddening, consuming need that spans the border between passion and indignation—I have never wanted to kiss someone who infuriates me so. It was your indifference to me, to my status. You were hell-bent on teaching me to be a better man whether you or I realised it."

Maribel squeezed his chest and bent to kiss him, and Thomas took advantage of the opportunity to turn her over, so it was he who now hovered above her. Their kiss deepened as her hands roamed his back, pulling the weight of his body down on her. He broke away panting, trying to catch his breath.

"Yes, Maribel, you have taught me much. I feel a heaviness lifted from my person, and that makes me smile with ease. And I now welcome your impertinence. But I still have many things to teach you, my sweet Maribel."

Her eyes were warm as toasted chestnuts as she looked up at him in capitulation, ready to be bent to his will.

"Then teach me." Her throaty response went straight to his loins and he groaned. Flipping them over again so she was straddling his waist, he pulled her thighs towards him, and she obeyed. He pulled her forward till she was straddling his face with her core directly over his mouth.

"My goodness, Thomas!" She gasped as he pressed his lips to that same spot. Maribel was shocked at the taboo gesture but revelled in it all the same. Clutching her plump cheeks, he nipped and tongued at her till she lost any shyness and began to writhe on his face. Now that he had driven her beyond reason, he broke his mouth free, peppering kisses to her thighs.

"Turn around, Maribel." His voice was guttural and half-pleading.

She obeyed wordlessly—all he could hear was her heavy breathing as she manoeuvred herself. Tracing his finger down the seam of her rear, he told her to lean forward. She needed no further instruction, and he felt her hands grasp his hard length.

"The student becomes the teacher," he purred, as he replaced his finger with his tongue and was rewarded with a shiver. Maribel, determined not to be outdone, took him into her mouth, using her tongue as she moved her head up and down. Thomas's last coherent thought was that the impertinent chit had taken the upper hand again, and a satisfied smile sprang to his lips. The world was quickly reduced to pleasures of the flesh, with hands, mouth, and tongue in a race to bring the most pleasure.

A race where everyone was a winner.

Chapter Nineteen

Maribel was finding it hard to focus on the day's lesson with Clara, after such a debauched evening and morning. But she was determined to separate her relationships with Thomas and Clara. And Clara deserved her full attention.

Today's lesson was at the pianoforte, and Clara's natural talent was shining through again as she played with the keys. Maribel was encouraging her to find her own sound, and Clara studiously concentrated on the tone of each key, making notes and murmuring to herself. Mr Whiskers sat beside her, currently grooming himself. Maribel could not help but smile at the pair who had bonded so seamlessly. She felt a pang of sadness that Mr Whiskers had found her so replaceable, but for the most part, she truly was happy with how events had played out.

And now I have Thomas.

Feeling a familiar blush heat her cheeks, she shook her head. Thomas was not her focus of the day. Her focus was her position as governess. One she was intent on keeping and performing well in, no matter the events that had transpired.

Any deep affection brewing inside her was for her alone to cope with. *A duke with a governess is just not done.*

Noise came from outside, and Maribel went to the window. A carriage was pulling up to the manor and staff were waiting outside.

"I wonder who that is?" she asked.

Clara, who had appeared beside her, was able to answer the question.

"My father's friend, the Duke of Lesterwich—that is his carriage."

Oh my, I will be in the presence of two dukes!

"Your father had not mentioned receiving any guest."

Clara shrugged and sat back down at the pianoforte.

"He and my father are always dropping in on one another. They are the best of friends. I just wish he had a child my age."

Following Clara's suit, Maribel took a seat and turned her attention back to the sound of music Clara was experimenting with.

🐈🐈🐈

"Good day, Lady Clara," came a deep drawl, and Maribel's head snapped up from the book she had been reading.

Clara stood and curtsied prettily and greeted the duke.

"And this is Lady Clara's governess, Miss Maribel Lewisham. Miss Lewisham, you have the honour of meeting my dear friend, the Duke of Lesterwich."

Maribel, following suit, gave a curtsey.

"Your Grace, it is an honour."

And certainly, it was—to be standing in the presence of two dukes, two very handsome dukes that were both eyeing her intensely. She suspected Thomas's friend knew who she was to him, and mortification brewed in her belly.

"Lady Clara and I do not mean to waylay you. We should be getting back to our lesson."

Maribel suspected taking charge was bold, but she needed distance, and thankfully, Thomas agreed. His friend looked at him with a mix of curiosity and amusement.

"You are correct, Miss Lewisham, it seems we have interrupted a musical lesson. I will leave you both."

He went to leave but turned back for a moment, tapping his fingers on the arch of the doorway.

"I would like Clara to join us for our meal later this evening—she can play for us. What do you think, Miss Lewisham?

"Yes, Your Grace, that is a fine idea."

As soon as the door was shut Clara and Maribel turned to each other.

"I better practice music for this eve—

"Let us change tact for the day—

They laughed over speaking at the exact same time.

"I think you should practice a sonata by Pleyel, a piece by Haydn for certain, and "Robin Adair" is always a popular tune."

Clara found the musical sheets and began to practice enthusiastically.

Maribel was pleased that Thomas had made the suggestion to include Clara. Her sweet face had lit up with joy at the invitation and proven that Thomas had been listening to Maribel. He was right—she *was* teaching him, and he was acting upon it. Taking her seat again, she listened to the music that filled the room and was content. A feeling she never would have expected to come from Thomas, recalling their first encounter and his stiff airs. Suppressing a laugh, she clapped at the end of Clara's song.

"Now a Haydn, Lady Clara. Bravo."

<h1 style="text-align:center">Chapter Twenty</h1>

Clara had made him very proud with her musical performance, and he continued to be impressed with the progress Maribel was making with his child. She had played beautifully, eaten her meal with pristine manners, and left to retire without a tantrum. Even Marcus was shocked, having known how Clara could be, and he lavished praise on Maribel's talents as a governess.

Thomas had forgotten how annoyingly charming Marcus was. The dashing rogue had arrived unannounced under the guise of wanting to check in on his friend. *Bah, more so that he was awash in curiosity to set eyes upon the woman who had tied me up in knots.*

"Why are you here, Marcus?" Those were the first words he had spoken to his friend when he had suddenly appeared in his drawing room.

"Is that any way to greet a friend?"

"Depends on my *friend's* motives as to why he has made the laborious trip from London."

"Well, besides my genuine need to ensure your wellbeing, I

will also admit that—given the twists and turns this woman had you in—I had to see her with my own eyes."

Thomas scowled and stood, waving a clenched fist in the air at his oldest and closest friend.

"She is not for you, Marcus. She is mine and mine alone."

"So, you bedded her?" Oh, how Thomas wanted to strike the smug look from his face.

"That is none of your business."

"Oh, really now? Since when do we not divulge to one another our dalliances?"

"She is not a dalliance!"

"She is at least twenty years your junior—what else could she be?"

Thomas was ready to spew a barrage of insults at his friend when he saw the twinkle in his eye. Marcus was baiting him. And he had fallen for it like the dolt he was.

"So, you are here to observe my descent into madness?"

"I guess love is a kind of madness."

"Love?" The word sounded foreign but was also a word that encompassed all the emotion building up inside him.

"How else can you explain it?"

The simple way Marcus spoke did not simplify his feelings. His heart was beating alarmingly fast, and a sweat had broken out on his palms.

How can I be in love with Maribel? Miss Lewisham, the governess?

"My brain is a mire! I cannot think!"

"Calm yourself, my friend, calm. Why don't you arrange for a scrumptious meal where you, Maribel, and I can get acquainted, and let me see if I can help you make sense of the situation?"

The lilt of Maribel's laugh broke through his reverie, and he glared at the pair who had warmed to one another instantly. Jealousy, a feeling previously as uncommon to him as love, now lurked in the pit of his stomach.

"You must have read more books than anyone else I have met, Miss Lewisham. It is no wonder you are drawn to teaching. How much knowledge you have to impart on the blank canvas that is youth."

Thomas watched her blush that pretty shade of rose he had come to adore because of the compliment paid by Marcus. It sickened him.

"If you two are done with your fawning, I would remind you both that I am also here."

Now he felt sickened by the petulance in his voice. He sounded worse than Clara on her worst day.

"I apologise, Your Grace." Maribel spoke politely, but her eyes shot daggers at him. Marcus, on the other hand, was trying to stifle a laugh.

They had been drinking port, except while Marcus had been taking mouthfuls, Maribel had been taking tiny sips. She always kept control of herself except in the throes of passion, which only he was now privy too. She still seemed vexed by him, and she narrowed her eyes in reprimand.

"Forgive me, Your Graces, I fear I must retire. I am overcome with tiredness. And I am sure you two have much to catch up on."

They bid her goodnight, and Thomas had no way to ask her to wait for him in his bed, so it appeared he would sleep alone tonight.

Turning to a gloating Marcus, he scowled.

"Explain yourself."

"I had to see that fine specimen of a woman for myself. You had left me so intrigued with your letter, your visit. I was worried she was some kind of charlatan intending to deceive you. I can see now that Maribel is a sweet woman—intelligent and a worthy opponent to challenge your flaws."

"Is that why you spent the evening flirting with her, you reprobate?"

"Ah, my friend, I did that purely for the joy of seeing your displeasure. Jealousy does not become you."

Still scowling, Thomas poured them another glass.

"Your timing is just very inconvenient. I am trying to determine how to navigate our situation. She has captured my very essence, and it is a feeling like no other. I want to be a good man—a man that's worthy of her."

"That is admirable, Thomas, but with all respect when I say this,—where can this go? She has no title, no land or money. A mistress or a companion is all I can see for her in your life."

"Where does it state that a duke cannot marry anyone he chooses?" he shot back hotly.

"It is not a written rule, but an unspoken one in our world. You know this, Thomas. And I quite like her, so believe me when I say it is a shame. You have much to consider and no need to make a decision now."

"You are correct. All that matters now is the now. And with that, I am also going to retire after this port. I believe I have had the perfect amount to allow me to sleep without agonising over the reality you just shared."

Chapter Twenty-One

Maribel had retired to bed, but after much deliberation, she relocated to Thomas's bed. Despite his provoking her ire with his childish behaviour, she wanted to be close to him. Too restless to fall asleep just yet, she was in front of his dressing room mirror. The frame was an ornate bronze that spoke of its expense. Maribel had wanted to stand nude in front of it but had not been brazen enough when Thomas was in the room. She had seen it when he had shown her the privy room behind it. He had then fascinated her with the news that his townhouse in London had recently had flushing toilets installed. She smiled to herself, recalling his amusement at her questions.

A lamp was burning, giving her enough light to see her figure, and she ran her fingers softly over her figure. Her plump curves had been worshipped by Thomas, and every inch of her person had felt cherished. Her breasts still felt heavy. Her nipples were the colour of dark honey surrounded by a lighter areola. The buds had hardened in arousal as her body responded to her wantonness. Her hair hung loose, and she recalled Thomas commenting how prettily the chestnut curls at her head matched the hair between her legs. It had never occurred to her a man could be so enraptured by every little detail. She moved her hands to the swell of her stomach.

Maribel heard breathing, and realising it wasn't hers, she diverted her gaze in the mirror and saw Thomas standing behind her in the dim light.

"You have no idea how relieved I am to see you standing here, Maribel. I had assumed you retired to your own bed."

He moved to stand behind her, his chest against her back, and grabbed her hands with his own. Using their hands, he began to stroke her, stopping at her breasts to fondle her stiffened nipples. A moan escaped at the erotic action of both their hands caressing her.

"It feels good, doesn't it, my sweet Maribel," he whispered while peppering kisses along the length of her neck and collarbone. She mewled in response, pressing her derrière against his crotch. Moving their hands further down, he traced the dip of her hips and the small of her stomach before reaching the spot that was most desperate for his touch. Still holding her hands in his own, he rubbed her mound, now moist with desire. It felt so deliciously wrong to have both their hands touching her in that place.

"How decadent, Thomas," she managed to gasp between quickened breaths.

"Yes, it is, and I am not done with you yet. Bend over and hold on to that chair over there and then spread your legs."

Asking no questions she quickly adopted the requested position while he undressed. Still behind her, he pulled her hips towards him, and she felt the length of him push inside her, pushing as deeply as he could, till she was certain that he filled every inch of her. She gripped the chair tightly with her hands and kept her feet planted firmly on the floor to take every thrust in stride.

"You are so very wilful, Maribel. You match me at every turn," he growled and spanked her bottom.

That sharp slap only heightened her desire.

"Do that again."

He spanked her other cheek so that both sides smarted, and he increased the pace of his movements, gripping her hips tightly. That familiar wave of ecstasy began to spread throughout her limbs, and the climax hit her quickly and forcefully as she tried to hold her balance.

"I have you, Maribel, take your pleasure," he cried as he joined her in release, pulling out and spending on her back.

Maribel felt at ease in Thomas's arms, but sleep eluded her. The aftermath of their passion was still humming in her veins. Turning to face him, she propped herself up on one arm, using the other to stroke that devilish grey streak.

"Thomas, are you still awake?"

"I am, Maribel, is something wrong?"

"I have been yearning to run my fingers through these grey strands."

"Is this why you woke me, to tell me I am an old man?" He asked in amusement.

"No, no, I am just reflecting on how content I feel. Though yes you are an old man," she teased.

"As do I. Between that unexpected release and all the port, I feel depleted and very relaxed. Could also be my age you minx."

"Why did you think I would not be waiting for you?"

"Because of my behaviour and your obvious annoyance. You do not have a subtle disposition, my sweet."

"Why, yes, I was annoyed at your silliness, but not enough to want to spend a night away from you. And it was kind of endearing, seeing you jealous. It had not occurred to me that you would prone to such an emotion."

"Usually I am not, but you are bringing out all kinds of new things in me, Miss Lewisham. Which Marcus was happy to point out," he added drily.

"Well, while I am not sure what this is between us, I do know we have plenty of time to understand it all. For now, I am simply content to fall asleep in your arms."

Thomas decided he would be guided by her. He had assumed she would be pressing him for clarity on the definition of their relationship, but if she was content to just enjoy the moments, so was he. They had plenty of time to discuss the future. And he could use this time to decide how he would navigate defying societal boundaries. Maribel was no commoner, but she still lacked any ties to the peerage. Pressing a kiss to her forehead, he closed his eyes and pushed away the thoughts. They had plenty of time to discuss the future. The word *future* evoked many pleasing thoughts. Maribel, his duchess. Mother to Clara. Belly rounded with their own baby.

"All in good time, my love," he whispered, comforted by her sweet breath.

Chapter Twenty-Two

Weeks later
Lovely sunlight beamed across the gardens, creating an idyllic setting for reading. Except Maribel was unable to focus on her book, for her thoughts could not be distracted from the unprecedented turn her life had taken. In the weeks since that first night of passion with Thomas, not a day had passed where they had not fallen asleep replete in one another's arms. By day, she went about her duty as governess, and by night, she and Thomas were ensconced in their own world—where they talked about everything except the future. As naive as Maribel knew she was being, she had refused to stray down that path. She knew what waited at the end of the trail. It was reality. A reality where she and a duke did not find a happily ever after. So, for now, ignorance was where she remained in bliss.

It had been an unusually quiet day where Maribel was able to relax in solitude. Clara was free to do as she pleased, Thomas had gone riding with Marcus, who was visiting, and she was lounging in a moment where she could simply be. Putting down her book, the works of John Donne, she stretched and moved her neck from side to side, hearing a satisfying crackle. Her stomach, not to be outdone, let out an audible grumble, demanding sustenance. Maribel set off for the kitchens, pulled by the freshly baked breads and pies she had smelled on her way to the gardens earlier. To enter the kitchens from outdoors, she needed to pass the laundry, and as she approached, she heard the chatter of young women. Maribel recognised the voices as Mary and Lucy, the scullery maids, and was about to announce herself when her name was mentioned. She took a step back and crouched behind a pile of chopped firewood outside the door.

"...if I had known His Grace was after a bed mate, I would have volunteered gladly."

"Aye, Maribel finds herself in luck, governess to whore. I would happily go from maid to whore. I am sick and tired of scrubbing the linens. My nails are worn down to ugly stubs!"

"Who is to say you would not still have to work? Maribel still carries out her governess duties?"

"I had not thought of that—she must enjoy her time with Lady Clara. The little brat has become much easier to manage."

"Maybe her thanks from His Grace was his taking her to bed." Lucy giggled and Maribel's face flamed.

"And she walks around all innocent, thinking she and His Grace are the only ones who know, when we all know what is taking place!"

"Aye, for a chit who Is meant to be a clever governess, she is certainly daft when it comes to being a canary bird."

"Surely she realises it's just a tup?"

"We will never know unless we ask, and I will do such thing. I will just wait till His Grace's eyes start to roam for something new."

The two women broke out in a twitter as Maribel broke out in a cold sweat. Humiliation rose from the depths of her stomach, and she placed her hand over her mouth, lest bilious shame spew forth. Hunger was now the furthest thing from her mind, so she scurried away as quickly and quietly as she could. The need for a haven from people who were laughing behind her back was the only need that mattered. Entering the manor, she dashed to her room and closed the door with a thump. Her heart raced, and the sick feeling had not abated as her mind whirled and repeated what she had heard.

I am naught but a fool, the greatest fool to ever live!

Maribel reprimanded herself over and over again, as if she was a student to her governess. A foolish child who had run headfirst into calamity and heeded no wisdom. The signs had always been there, but she had chosen to ignore them. Thomas had always seen her as simply a governess. His transformation from stern aloofness to adoring suitor had been built on lust, not love. She had been only too eager to experience his touch, to stoke the flames burning uncontrollably on the pyre of their desire.

Shame on me for caterwauling all these nights!

A scratching at the door interrupted her self-depreciation, and she opened it to find Mr Whiskers waiting, concern etched upon his furry face.

"My dear four-legged friend, come in. You sensed my distress, my woe at playing the fool. I took this position to prove my worth as a governess. I brought you along so I would not be alone. And now I must go, and you must stay, as I could not bear to break Clara's heart. Especially now that I know what a heart bursting with sadness feels like."

As always, he stared back with comprehension and affectionately rubbed his face on her feet. Maribel sat on the floor and pulled him into her arms. The vibration of his purr had always induced a calming effect, and she needed to think clearly. She could not stay. She could not discuss this with Thomas—he would try and convince her to stay and continue as his mistress. Why would he not, after she had made it so easy? Perhaps that's what had allured him, the satisfaction of having her capitulate. No, she could not stay. She would leave him a note. The words would be written straight from the depths of her heart. She needed to return home and regroup and perhaps seek a position abroad. Soon enough the gossip would follow her, and it would only shame her family. She cringed at the disappointment all five brothers would feel. She was their Mari, sharp-minded, sharp-tongued. Never would she fall into the traps laid by men. But she had. And now only she could mend her future that hung so precariously in the balance. Shifting Mr Whiskers from her lap, she moved to her desk and picked up her quill and paper. A droplet of liquid fell to the parchment and Maribel lifted a hand to her eyes. She had not felt the tears that had welled up and now sought escape. Blinking, she gave the salty sadness free passage to run down her face as she wrote her goodbyes.

<h1 style="text-align:center">Chapter Twenty-Three</h1>

Thomas heard a roaring. An enraged bellow echoed through his bedroom. Was a wild beast loose in his manor? No, it was he who was the beast, a wounded beast. Waiting for him on his bed—a bed where Maribel had recently spent all her nights—was a letter. His ride had turned into a hunting trip, and he had been gone for two evenings and was desperate to see her. Marcus had taunted him relentlessly. It was late, so he had gone to her room, which was oddly bare. He asked his staff, who shook their heads, their eyes wide with trepidation. Hope that she was waiting for him in his bed had been his only solace before reading the saddest words he had ever seen written.

> Dearest Thomas,
>
> I write to you in deep sorrow, and much as it pains me to share this, with regret.
>
> The employment opportunity as governess to Lady Clara has proven to be a truly enlightening

and satisfying experience. I feel in such a short time that Lady Clara has gone from strength to strength, and in large part this was due to her willingness to make changes. And because you also decided to make changes.

My time spent with you these last few weeks has also brought me much joy. You changed from the stern duke I first encountered to a man of tolerance and liberality, and it gives me pride that I managed to teach you something as well.

Alas, our idyllic time must come to an end, as we both knew it would. You have reminded me repeatedly I am simply a governess, and I never forgot you are a duke, except perhaps in those moments when I called you Thomas. We were two fools engaged in play, a play we wrote with each passing day while deliberately ignoring the reality that awaited us at the end. Which is where we now are. In time, I am sure I will remember this interlude fondly, but at this present time, the severity of my actions weighs heavily upon my chest. Our passion is no secret, and secrets spread. I will not allow my family to incur such shame by my remaining here, so please accept my resignation as governess. I have decided to start anew abroad, and with the passing of time, my heart will surely heal.

My only request is for you to continue to give Clara the love and attention she deserves. I have left Mr Whiskers with her, so please be kind to him also. She will be more reliant on him now than ever.

Miss Maribel Lewisham

What in the blazes did this all mean? She had left him? Secrets? Regrets? Moving abroad? How absurd! Did that impertinent chit really believe they had been fools? Questions raced through his mind as he fingered the smudged ink spots. He knew they were her tears, and he felt his own heart split in two.

"Thomas, I heard you roar, and I am hoping I have allowed enough time for you to compose yourself so I may enter." Marcus's concerned voice came through the closed door.

Thomas opened it and threw the letter at his friend in defeat. He watched Marcus scan the lines, his brow raising higher with each sentence till they were hidden by his hair. Seeing Marcus was equally surprised at the content of the letter made him feel a tiny bit better. It proved he was not the only one to have missed the signs.

"I am in shock. Something must have occurred while we were gone?" Marcus queried, still evidently puzzled.

"Indeed, but instead of waiting to discuss it with me, she took off like the stubborn chit she has always been," Thomas raged.

"Perhaps, but this does not mean the end, Thomas, if you calm down and think rationally. Go to her and see how and what can be remedied. You just spent the last two days telling me you had decided to wed her. Surely you are just not going to give up?"

"Wed her? She ran out on me!"

"Think, Thomas, think. It sounds to me like time has caught up with her. The guilt, the shame. She isn't a seasoned mistress or a three-penny upright! And to be fair, you had not shared your intentions with her. You can be quite maddening, Thomas. If I was a woman, I would surely not put up with you."

"You think I should make my way to her home? I know where she lives, her family home." The formulation of a plan started to calm him down and clear his. His friend was right. This does not mean the end. He could make this right.

"I think you should, but firstly, I think you should get a good night's rest. Then head out first thing in the morning. I will stay and care take things for you and pray I see you both return. You would be fools to let the opportunity of lifelong happiness slip between your fingers out of misunderstanding. And do not forget, arrogance has always been a flaw of yours."

Thomas waved off the insult, knowing Marcus spoke true. He would get some rest and be ready to travel to Cheltenshire at first light.

Chapter Twenty-Four

Maribel had no regret about grabbling one of Thomas's carriages. It would return to him after she returned home. That was the least he could provide. It would take her days to return home by foot, and she wanted distance between herself and that damned man as soon as possible. Maribel knew she had not been blameless in the situation, but directing her anger towards him assuaged her own guilt. Her penance was leaving Mr Whiskers behind, which made the pang in her chest ache anew.

"Lady Clara, I need to return home immediately."

"Why Miss Lewisham? Did something happen to your family?" Clara's blue eyes widened with alarm.

"No, no, that is not why. I just need to return. It is hard to explain."

Clara looked confused and hurt, and it made Maribel feel awful to know she was the cause of her feeling suddenly abandoned.

Clara had thrown the book she was holding to the ground and stomped her little feet in the full throes of a tantrum that they had worked so hard to get past. All their work was now undone with her simple decision, selfish or not, to abandon the young child.

But how could she tell the young girl that she now paid the price for partaking in a cardinal sin? And even more harrowing was the realisation that she would need to leave Mr Whiskers. She could not leave the child and take her newfound friend too.

I am leaving behind a life I have come to cherish, but this is the price I must pay for my impulsivity.

The memory made her eyes burn with tears. Lady Clara had claimed a part of her heart also.

The carriage arrived at her family home, and without waiting for any assistance, she stepped down, asking the driver to leave her belongings by the fence as she picked up her skirts and ran towards the home.

"Mother, Mother, I have returned home!" she yelled, knowing her mother could be anywhere this time of day.

"Mari, why are you here?" asked Richard, the first to meet her.

"No warm greeting or embrace for your sister?" she reprimanded in reply as she pulled him close. The scent of lavender from his head comforted her as she squeezed him tight.

"Mari, what a surprise!" Her mother rushed over to give her a hug.

"A surprise I hope you are all happy for! The family will all be here for dinner tonight, yes?"

It was a tradition for the Lewishams to share their evening meal together at least once a week. Her older brothers always returned home, and the only exceptions had been made for Mari and her father if work was pressing.

"It is. Your brothers will be here soon, but your father is unfortunately away in London. Why don't you freshen up and then join me in the kitchen."

Relieved she was not yet being peppered with questions, she did as her mother said and immediately felt the comfort of her old room, where life had been much simpler. Curling up in a ball on her bed, she closed her eyes and allowed the familiar surroundings to soothe her weary soul.

***

"Maribel, my dear, it is time to wake up." Maribel opened her eyes to see her mother smiling down at her, a hint of concern on her face.

"Did I fall asleep?"

"You did, and you looked so peaceful that I am only waking you up now to eat."

"I will be down in a moment. Tell the boys I will be quick. I know how eager their bellies are!"

Splashing water on her face and smoothing her hair, she slipped on her shoes and made her way to the dining room. John, Matthew, Liam, Richard, and Frederick stood as she entered the room and greeted them one by one with a warm embrace and they all began to speak at once.

"What was the duke like?"

"Why are you home?"

"Was your charge kind?"

"What did they feed you?"

"Was the estate filled with riches?"

"Where is Mr Whiskers?"

"Boys, let your sister sit down, and ask her questions one by one, not all at once!"

Maribel laughed so heartily it filled the void of despair she had come to know in the past few days. The mayhem of her family was a balm to her soul.

"The duke was stern initially, but did soften in time. I am home as I plan on seeking a governess role abroad. My student, Lady Clara, was delightful after a bumpy start. They fed me the same food we eat here—that was an odd question, Fred— and the manor was richly furnished, but I would not say filled with riches. And Mr Whiskers decided to stay, as he has found a new companion in Lady Clara."

The answers to their questions only led to another barrage of questions, including one from her mother, which was the one she answered.

"Abroad, Mari? Are you ready for such a big leap?" Her mother's brow furrowed.

"I am. I have learned much, and while England will always be home, I want new experiences." Now was not the time to tell her mother the real reason she wanted to flee. She was dreading that conversation but knew it would have to be had before the gossip spread.

"Enough about me! Tell me, John and Matthew, how do your studies fare? And Liam, you are looking very holy. And you two scoundrels, have you been keeping up with your lessons?"

The familiar chaos of home and family achieved the miracle of making her forget her own plight. Maribel had forgotten how it was to feel before she had ever encountered the duke, and a night like this was just what she'd needed.

Chapter Twenty-Five

The decision between the speed of mounting a horse to gallop at pace and the practicality of a carriage drew out as he paced back and forth. His stable master struggled to keep his expression neutral. The poor man had already endured a tirade when he informed Thomas that it was he who had arranged for Maribel's departure.

Left me no choice, she was most insistent, Thomas recalled his defence.

While he wanted to be mad at the man for abetting her abandonment, he begrudgingly admitted that Maribel would have been most insistent and hard to refuse.

Thomas decided on the carriage for practicality, since Maribel *would* be returning with him. Journeying this way left him with time to ponder, and with each passing moment, he felt more unease. What if she said no? What if she had already left? Gazing out the window nauseated him, but he refused to tear his eyes away, knowing the town of Cheltenshire would soon come into view. He had never been there, but it was close to his country estate, and he had tenants sprinkled about. It occurred to him how little he had showed his face to his neighbours and tenants, and he was indeed one of the most priggish of his peers. Houses began to appear in view, and he sat up and tried to compose his expression, imagining he looked like an eager boy rather than the esteemed Duke of Avondale. He nodded to a farmer who gaped at him and smiled at a woman carrying a basket of goods, who blushed in surprise. He even found himself waving at a group of young lads who ran alongside the carriage.

Perhaps I should visit the townspeople more often, he thought, enjoying the interactions.

The carriage suddenly veered to the right, and he could see a dwelling in the distance—a decent-sized home, aged but sturdily built. Two young boys were watching the carriage pull up, probably Maribel's young brothers, as he noted they were identical. The carriage pulled to a stop, and he exited without waiting for his man to open the door.

"Good day, young fellows. I have come to call on Miss Maribel Lewisham."

"Who are you? What do you want with our Mari?"

Impertinence is apparently a family trait, he thought drily.

"Boys, that is no way to address a guest. My apologies, sir, I am Mrs Lewisham. Who should I tell Maribel is calling?"

The woman was an older, softer version of Maribel—grey strands spun through her brown hair, and her chestnut eyes shone with warmth.

"Oh, yes, pardon me, I am yet to introduce myself. I am Thomas Denby, the Duke of Avondale."

Mrs Lewisham gasped but recovered quickly and, remembering her manners, gave a small curtsey.

"Mari said she doesn't work for you?" one of the boys asked, clearly nonplussed by his status.

"Boys, hush. Go get Mari." Mrs Lewisham shooed them away before turning back to him. "Your Grace, please come inside and let me provide refreshment for you both."

Thomas had forgotten that Mal was behind him until Mrs. Lewisham tried to usher them both in, but Mal politely declined in order to stay with the horses. Thomas was glad, he didn't need his man to see him grovel. Because he would, if that's what it came to.

Taking a seat in a small parlour, he looked around the inviting space that Maribel called home. As promised, Mrs Lewisham returned with tea and a plate of biscuits that looked freshly baked. As he was thanking her, he heard Maribel's voice.

"Your Grace, what an unexpected surprise."

"I shall leave you both to talk."

Thinking it odd that her mother would leave them unchaperoned but grateful all the same, he stood and reached out to Maribel. She was unmoved, with her arms crossed and eyes narrowed. She was every inch the stern and resilient governess he had sought.

"Maribel, I have been a fool."

"As have I. But unlike you, I have taken the necessary steps to remedy the situation."

"By running away?"

"I am protecting my family from gossip. Well, I cannot spare them from it, but I can ensure I am not around to make matters worse."

"What gossip? Why are you so infuriating?" He heard the edge in his voice but did not care. Maribel was so aloof—every word she spoke an assault on his heart.

"That I, the simple governess from Cheltenshire, played mistress to the Duke of Avondale. Your scullery maids were discussing it openly. It was only a matter of time. And I cannot blame you in full—we both made the choice to dally with one another without the promise of it becoming anything else."

Suddenly, it all made sense. She had overheard gossip—he

made a note to seriously reprimand them both—and had taken it upon herself to make the best of a bad situation. Or so she thought.

"Maribel, I wish you had waited. Had come to me. Because while I was gone with Marcus, I had come to a decision. One that impacts you, my simple little governess."

Her eyes shot daggers at his choice of words, and he smiled at her ire.

"I will not be your mistress! I have confessed the true events to my mother, and she supports my decision to move abroad. I would not dare seek her support to lower myself to be your mistress."

"For a clever woman, you are being quite dicked in the nob!" He raised his voice.

"Do not insult me in my own home!"

"Why not? You never held back in my home!"

"Why are you even here, Your Grace, surely this is beneath you!"

"I am here because I love you, you sharp-tongued shrew, and I want to marry you!"

"Oh."

"Can I kiss you now, or would you like to argue some more?"

"Kiss me, Thomas, kiss me now and forever."

"It is not only I who will need to be appeased," Thomas told her. The carriage was nearing home, and he gave her shoulder a reassuring squeeze, his arm draped around her.

"I know. Is Clara still very cross?"

"Cross, upset, angry. And not just with you but myself as well. Naturally, she has blamed me for everything."

"It truly clawed at my heart to say goodbye to her."

"That is the past now, sweet Maribel. You are her present, you are her future, and I am certain that will be enough to gain her forgiveness."

Surely enough, Clara waited for them at the open door, Mr Whiskers by her side. They both showed looks of scorn, the sting of her abandonment apparently still fresh. Maribel leaped from the carriage and ran to the pair. Pulling Clara under one arm and Mr Whiskers under the other she squeezed them with all her might.

"I am so sorry for the pain I have caused. I promise I will never leave again."

"I guess we can forgive you, Miss Mari, but to be certain you do not do it again, I think you should write a letter of apology."

Thomas bit his lip to refrain from smiling.

"You are absolutely correct. I should, and I will."

Clara turned to Mr Whiskers and gave a nod of approval.

"If you have promised to never leave again, does this mean you will stay as my governess?"

"Well Clara, I have asked Maribel to marry me, so she will be your mother."

Clara squealed in delight, clapping her tiny hands together.

"That means you can never leave me!"

"I am glad you feel this way, Clara, and I may become your mother, but I will still be your governess. To be learned is to be wise, Clara."

"I have much more to learn, so I am very pleased, Mama Mari."

Her address melted the last ice chip lurking in Thomas's

heart. His family was whole, even if it included that wretched feline who watched him smugly.

"And I am glad to hear no objection from you, Thomas—I will be mother, governess, and then duchess."

"You will hear none from me—the governess is who I fell in love with, and you are a mother I will continue to fall in love with every day. It is the greatest of honours that I can also call you my duchess."

Scooping Clara and Maribel into his arms, he held them both tight.

"I will ensure only happy smiles dance upon both your faces, my loves."

Epilogue

The wedding of Miss Maribel Lewisham and Thomas Denby, the Duke of Avondale, would leave the ton with a never-ending source of gossip. Behind their backs anyhow. It would also leave a slew of untitled young ladies with the hope that they, too, could one day find the love of a duke. Maribel had insisted their nuptials be quick and without fuss, which is how they found themselves at Gretna Green. Thomas disliked Scotland, so Maribel had found it very amusing how eager he had been to arrive here. The Lewishams, Marcus, and Clara—with Mr Whiskers, of course —had come to bear witness.

Maribel was grateful for Clara's ecstatic response to Mari becoming a mother figure and still remaining a teacher—they had hugged off and on for hours. Maribel had pulled Thomas aside to make him promise that he would allow Maribel to continue teaching. It was not only a means of employ but her burning passion to impart knowledge. Thomas had promised to give her many babies so she would not lack for students. She could not help but adore that roguish wit. Her reminiscence was shattered by a cacophony of voices, and her gaze settled on the scene before her. The Lewishams were boisterous, and Maribel was grateful they were the only patrons.

Her brothers were in awe that their Mari was marrying a duke, but only when Thomas was not around, as to his face, they continued to lack any kind of manners. This drove their mother crazy and she made constant apologies that Thomas kept brushing off.

Marcus had taken it upon himself to be the teller of their story, one in which their union had come to pass mainly through his efforts, which Thomas rebuked at every turn.

For privacy, Thomas had paid for every room in the inn, so it was only their families and Marcus. Her three older brothers hung on every word he spoke, while the twins and Clara ran wild playing all kind of games. Maribel had never had a more perfect moment with all the people that she loved. Seated between her mother and Thomas, they waited for her father to arrive, and the following morning, they would be wed! Thomas kept calling her his duchess, and she swatted him on the arm each time. She may be almost a duchess, but she was always Maribel and always would be. She would continue to teach Clara. And continue to teach Thomas. No matter her title.

"Maribel was always my easiest child—from the time she was a wee babe, she was calm, decisive, and eager to learn. My boys, on the other hand, were a rambunctious lot until they became men. So I do have hope for young Frederick and Richard." The latter was currently jumping off a chair, with Clara about to follow suit.

"As unladylike as my daughter is behaving, I admit it warms my heart to see her overjoyed and playful with children similar in age. We may need to have a baby sooner rather than later, Maribel."

"Thomas!" she gasped. "Not in front of my mother," she added in a whisper.

"She has birthed six children, my sweet, I am certain she knows how babies are made," he whispered back wickedly.

Maribel had made him pledge they would not make love again till they were wed, and instead, she had been subject to many wicked comments. Little did he know that she and her mother had learned a secret in the last sennight—she was already with child! It would be her wedding gift to him. A gift of what their love had created. When she had taught a duke how to love without restraint and expectations. Just to love with all his heart.

A note for you darling reader

Dear reader

Thank you once again for taking your time to read Thomas & Maribel's story!

It is hard to express how utterly thrilled and honoured I am to be involved in the Wayward Duke Alliance with the host of exceptionally talented writers in this series!

As soon as I joined up, the title 'The Governess Teaches A Duke" sprung to mind and I worked from there, wanting a stuffy hero and a strong heroine. Elements of including a 'soon to be step-child' and 'age gap' are not ones I generally include in my stories which also added a layer of fun! This novella of mine allowed me to explore my writing creativity and I truly hope you enjoyed the words.

Taking a journey to Regency England is always a wonderful time especially the research. Governesses, furniture, word entomology of the time and those fantastic words/phrases we rarely, if at all hear or say anymore!

To name a few:

- *Dicked in the nob - silly, crazy, foolish*
- *Dimber - pretty, neat*
- *On-dit - gossip*
- *Too high in the instep - proud, haughty, snobbish*
- *Goosecap - silly person*

Love Steffy xxx

WD
The Governess
A Teaches
Duke
STEFFY SMITH

About the Author

Steffy is forever reading, forever dreaming. And mainly, forever wishing she was dancing at a Regency Ball, drinking *uisge beatha* in a medieval Scottish keep, navigating a Norman-Saxon romance, or riding up on horseback into a Western town.

Follow her writing journey, as one by one these stories will unfold. To be kept informed of new releases, updates, and most importantly to connect with any feedback or reviews, please sign up to her newsletter at www.steffysmithbooks.com.

Steffy Smith

Natural Impatience and Righteous Indignation

Regency Runaway Brides
Regina Is Out Of Luck
STEFFY SMITH

Also by Steffy Smith

An English Garden
(Georgian England)
A Marquess of Roses
An Earl of Bluebells (
*A Viscount of Lavender (coming 2026)**
*A Baron of Thistles (coming 2027)**

Highland Hearts
(Medieval Scotland)
The Bonniest Lass in Scotland
Highland Heartbreaker
*Book III (coming 2027)**

Curves&Cravats
(Regency England)
His Regency Goddess

Romancing the Rake Anthology
The Widow Reforms A Rake
(Regency England Short)

Lore & Love Trilogy
(Viking Age)
Her Viking Saviour
*Spring Maiden (coming 2026)**
*Viking in Love (coming 2027)**

Suffragette Uprising

Natural Impatience & Righteous Indignation (Coming 2026)

Regency Runaway Brides

Regina is Out of Luck (coming 2026)

**Publication year subject to change.*

Steffy Smith Books